Dieses Buch beginnt mit den berühmten Worten:

Once upon a time there were four little rabbits, and
their names were Flopsy, Mopsy, Cottontail, and
Peter. They lived with their mother in a sand-bank,
underneath the root of a very big fir-tree.

In schönem ganz leichtem Englisch werden aufregende – immer gut ausgehende – Geschichten
erzählt, in diesem Band vier kurze und eine (besonders
aufregende) lange. Die Kaninchen (auf deutsch heißen
sie Hoppeli, Poppeli, Wattepusch und natürlich Peter)
kommen in jeder dieser Geschichten vor. Außerdem
treten auf: Das Kaninchen Benjamin Purzel und seine
Familie; die Igelfrau Mrs Tiggy-winkle (Frau Pieke-
Schnack); der Fuchs Mr Tod (Junker Voss); der Dachs
Tommy Brock (Meister Gräving); der Gärtner Mr
McGregor (Herr Gregerich); das Bauernmädchen
Lucie (natürlich Lucie) sowie einige Tierlein am Rande:
Katze, Maus, Henne, Rotkehlchen . . .

Englischer Text und deutsche Übersetzung stehen
einander fast zeilengleich gegenüber.

Beatrix Potter wurde 1866 geboren. Mit 29 Jahren
schrieb und zeichnete sie «Peter Rabbit» für den fünf-
jährigen Sohn ihrer einstigen Gouvernante. 1902 kam
«Peter Rabbit» als Buch heraus, im Verlag ihres früh
verstorbenen Verlobten Frederick Warne. Das Büch-
lein wurde ein großer Erfolg, und nun schrieb Beatrix
Potter Geschichte um Geschichte – insgesamt rund
dreißig. 1913 hörte sie auf zu schreiben. Sie heiratete
und widmete sich fortan dem Bauernhof, den sie sich
gekauft hatte. 1943 starb sie, betrauert von vielen
Millionen jungen und irgendwann mal jung gewesenen
Lesern ihrer Bücher in aller Welt.

dtv zweisprachig · Edition Langewiesche-Brandt

Beatrix Potter

Peter Rabbit and other tales

Peter Karnickel und andere Geschichten

Übersetzung von Angela Uthe-Spencker

Deutscher Taschenbuch Verlag

Zeichnungen nach den farbigen Bildern der Autorin
von Magelone Richter

Neuübersetzung
1. Auflage November 1994
Rechte an der Übersetzung:
Deutscher Taschenbuch Verlag GmbH & Co. KG, München
Umschlagentwurf: Celestino Piatti
Satz: FoCoTex Klaus Nowak, Berg bei Starnberg
Gesamtherstellung: Kösel, Kempten
ISBN 3-423-09322-6. Printed in Germany

The Tale of Peter Rabbit

Die Geschichte von Peter Karnickel

Once upon a time there were four little Rabbits, and their names were – Flopsy, Mopsy, Cottontail, and Peter. They lived with their Mother in a sand-bank, underneath the root of a very big fir-tree.

"Now, my dears," said old Mrs Rabbit one morning, "you may go into the fields or down the lane, but don't go into Mr McGregor's garden: your Father had an accident there; he was put in a pie by Mrs McGregor. "Now run along, and don't get into mischief. I am going out."

Then old Mrs Rabbit took a basket and her umbrella, and went through the wood to the baker's. She bought a loaf of brown bread and five currant buns.

Flopsy, Mopsy, and Cottontail, who were good little bunnies, went down the lane to gather blackberries. But Peter, who was very

Es waren einmal vor langer Zeit vier kleine Karnickel. Sie hießen Hoppeli, Poppeli, Wattepusch und Peter. Sie wohnten zusammen mit ihrer Mutter in einem sandigen Abhang unter der Wurzel einer sehr großen Kiefer.

«Also, meine Lieben», sagte eines Morgens Mutter Karnickel, «ihr dürft auf die Äcker gehen oder den Feldweg entlang, doch wagt euch nicht in den Garten von Herrn Gregerich. Euer Vater hatte dort einen Unfall. Er wurde von Frau Gregerich in eine Pastete gefüllt. Nun trollt euch und stellt keine Dummheiten an. Ich mache mich jetzt auf den Weg.»

Dann nahm Mutter Karnickel Einkaufskorb und Regenschirm und ging durch den Wald zum Bäcker. Sie kaufte einen Laib Schwarzbrot und fünf Korinthenbrötchen.

Hoppeli, Poppeli und Wattepusch, die artige Kaninchen waren, gingen den Feldweg entlang, um Brombeeren zu sammeln. Aber Peter, der sehr unfolgsam

naughty, ran straight away to Mr McGregor's garden, and squeezed under the gate!

First he ate some lettuces and some French beans; and then he ate some radishes. And then, feeling rather sick, he went to look for some parsley.

But round the end of a cucumber frame, whom should he meet but Mr McGregor!

Mr McGregor was on his hands and knees planting out young cabbages, but he jumped up and ran after Peter, waving a rake and calling out, "Stop thief!"

Peter was most dreadfully frightened; he rushed all over the garden, for he had forgotten the way back to the gate. He lost one of his shoes among the cabbages, and the other shoe amongst the potatoes.

After losing them, he ran on four legs and went faster, so that I think he might have got away altogether if he had not unfortunately run into a gooseberry net, and got caught by the large buttons on his jacket. It was a blue jacket with brass buttons, quite new.

war, lief flink davon zum Garten von Herrn Gregerich und zwängte sich unterm Gatter hindurch.

Erst aß er ein paar Salatblätter und einige Feuerbohnen. Dann aß er ein paar Radieschen. Und dann, weil ihm ziemlich übel war, ging er auf die Suche nach etwas Petersilie.

Doch hinter dem anderen Ende eines Frühbeetes mit Gurken, wen traf er da? Natürlich Herrn Gregerich!

Herr Gregerich lag auf den Knien und pflanzte Kohlsetzlinge ins Freiland. Aber jetzt sprang er auf und lief hinter Peter her, wobei er eine Harke schwang und rief: «Haltet den Dieb!»

Peter fürchtete sich entsetzlich. Er flitzte wild im Garten herum, denn er hatte den Weg zurück zum Gatter vergessen. Er verlor den einen Schuh zwischen den Kohlpflanzen und den anderen inmitten der Kartoffeln.

Nachdem er beide verloren hatte, lief er auf allen Vieren und darum schneller, so daß ich glaube, er wäre bestimmt entkommen – wenn er nicht leider in ein Stachelbeernetz geraten und mit den großen Knöpfen seiner Jacke hängengeblieben wäre. Es war eine blaue Jacke mit Messingknöpfen, noch ganz neu.

Peter gave himself up for lost, and shed big tears; but his sobs were overheard by some friendly sparrows, who flew to him in great excitement, and implored him to exert himself.

Mr McGregor came up with a sieve, which he intended to pop upon the top of Peter; but Peter wriggled out just in time, leaving his jacket behind him. And rushed into the toolshed, and jumped into a can. It would have been a beautiful thing to hide in, if it had not had so much water in it.

Mr McGregor was quite sure that Peter was somewhere in the tool-shed, perhaps hidden underneath a flowerpot. He began to turn them over carefully, looking under each.

Presently Peter sneezed – "Kertyschoo!" Mr McGregor was after him in no time. And tried to put his foot upon Peter, who jumped out of a window, upsetting three plants. The

Peter glaubte, daß alles aus sei, und vergoß dicke Tränen. Doch sein Geschluchze wurde von einigen freundlichen Sperlingen gehört, die in großer Aufregung zu ihm schwirrten und ihn beschworen, nichts unversucht zu lassen.

Herr Gregerich kam mit einem Sieb angerannt, das er Peter überstülpen wollte. Doch Peter konnte sich gerade noch herauswinden, indem er seine Jacke zurückließ. Er sauste in den Geräteschuppen und hopste in eine Gießkanne. Sie wäre ein wunderschönes Versteck gewesen, wenn nicht so viel Wasser drin gewesen wäre.

Herr Gregerich war überzeugt, daß Peter irgendwo im Schuppen war, vielleicht unter einem Blumentopf versteckt. Er begann die Blumentöpfe vorsichtig umzudrehen und schaute unter jeden einzelnen.

Da mußte Peter gerade niesen: «Hatschi!» Herr Gregerich war im Nu bei ihm. Er versuchte seinen Fuß auf Peter zu setzen, doch der sprang aus dem Fenster und warf dabei drei Topfpflanzen um. Das Fenster war

window was too small for Mr McGregor, and he was tired of running after Peter. He went back to his work.

Peter sat down to rest; he was out of breath and trembling with fright, and he had not the least idea which way to go. Also he was very damp with sitting in that can.

After a time he began to wander about, going lippity – lippity – not very fast, and looking all round. He found a door in a wall; but it was locked, and there was no room for a fat little rabbit to squeeze underneath.

An old mouse was running in and out over the stone door-step, carrying peas and beans to her family in the wood. Peter asked her the way to the gate, but she had such a large pea in her mouth that she could not answer. She only shook her head at him. Peter began to cry.

für Herrn Gregerich zu eng. Auch hatte er es satt, hinter Peter herzulaufen. Er ging zurück an seine Arbeit.

Peter setzte sich erst einmal, um zu verschnaufen. Er war außer Atem, zitterte vor Angst und hatte nicht die geringste Ahnung, in welche Richtung er laufen sollte. Auch war er durch den Aufenthalt in der Gießkanne sehr feucht.

Nach einer Weile begann er umherzugehen; er ging – hoppeldi-hoppeldi – nicht sehr schnell und schaute sich oft um. Er fand eine Tür in einer Mauer. Doch sie war verschlossen, und für ein dickes kleines Kaninchen war nicht genug Platz, sich durchzuzwängen.

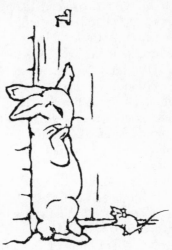

Eine alte Maus lief rein und raus über die steinerne Türschwelle und trug Erbsen und Bohnen zu ihrer Familie in den Wald. Peter fragte sie nach dem Weg zum Gatter, doch die Maus hatte so eine große Erbse im Mund, daß sie nicht antworten konnte. Sie schüttelte nur den Kopf über Peter. Peter begann zu weinen.

Then he tried to find his way straight across the garden, but he became more and more puzzled. Presently, he came to a pond where Mr McGregor filled his water-cans. A white cat was staring at some gold-fish, she sat very, very still, but now and then the tip of her tail twitched as if it were alive. Peter thought it best to go away without speaking to her; he had heard about cats from his cousin, little Benjamin Bunny.

He went back towards the toolshed, but suddenly, quite close to him, he heard the noise of a hoe – scr-r-ritch, scratch, scratch, scritch. Peter scuttered underneath the bushes. But presently, as nothing happened, he came out, and climbed upon a wheelbarrow and peeped over. The first thing he saw was Mr McGregor hoeing onions. His back was turned towards Peter, and beyond him was the gate!

Peter got down very quietly off the wheelbarrow, and started running as fast as he could go, along a straight walk behind some blackcurrant bushes.

Mr McGregor caught sight of him at the corner, but Peter did not care. He slipped underneath the gate, and was safe at last in the wood outside the garden.

Mr McGregor hung up the little jacket and the shoes for a scarecrow to frighten the blackbirds.

Peter never stopped running or looked behind him till he got home to the big fir-tree.

He was so tired that he flopped down upon the nice soft sand on the floor of the rabbit-hole and shut his eyes. His mother was busy

Dann versuchte er stracks quer durch den Garten seinen Weg zu finden, doch er geriet immer mehr durcheinander. Bald kam er an einen Teich, aus dem Herr Gregerich immer seine Gießkannen füllte. Eine weiße Katze starrte auf ein paar Goldfische, sie saß vollkommen reglos, nur hin und wieder zuckte ihre Schwanzspitze, als wäre die lebendig. Peter hielt es für das Beste, sich davonzumachen, ohne sie anzusprechen. Er hatte von seinem Vetter, dem kleinen Benjamin Purzel, einiges über Katzen gehört.

Er ging wieder zum Geräteschuppen hin. Da vernahm er plötzlich ganz in seiner Nähe das Geräusch einer Hacke – schirr, scharr, scharr, schirr. Peter flitzte unter die Büsche. Doch da nichts geschah, kam er kurz darauf wieder hervor, kletterte auf eine Schubkarre und äugte hinüber. Als erstes sah er Herrn Gregerich, der im Zwiebelbeet hackte. Sein Rücken war Peter zugewandt, und jenseits von ihm befand sich das Gatter!

Peter kroch ganz leise von der Schubkarre herunter und sauste dann so schnell er konnte hinter einigen Büschen Schwarze Johannisbeeren einen geraden Pfad entlang.

Herr Gregerich erblickte ihn am Ende des Pfades, doch Peter kümmerte es nicht. Er schlüpfte unter dem Gatter hindurch und war endlich sicher im Wald außerhalb des Gartens.

Herr Gregerich hängte die kleine Jacke und die Schuhe als Vogelscheuche auf, um die Amseln abzuschrecken.

Peter hörte nicht auf zu laufen und sah sich nicht um, bis er zu Hause an der großen Kiefer angelangt war.

Er war so müde, daß er auf den wohligen weichen Sand am Boden des Kaninchenbaus niederplumpste und die Augen schloß. Seine Mutter war mit Kochen

cooking; she wondered what he had done with his clothes. It was the second little jacket and pair of shoes that Peter had lost in a fortnight!

I am sorry to say that Peter was not very well during the evening. His mother put him to bed, and made some camomile tea; and she gave a dose of it to Peter! "One table-spoonful to be taken at bed-time."

But Flopsy, Mopsy, and Cottontail had bread and milk and blackberries for supper.

beschäftigt. Sie fragte sich, was er mit seinen Kleidern angestellt hatte. Es war die zweite kleine Jacke und das zweite Paar Schuhe, die Peter innerhalb von vierzehn Tagen verloren hatte.

Leider muß ich erzählen, daß es Peter an diesem Abend nicht besonders gut ging. Seine Mutter steckte ihn ins Bett und goß ein wenig Kamillentee auf. Ein bißchen davon gab sie Peter zu schlucken. «Man nehme einen Eßlöffel vorm Schlafengehen!»

Hoppeli, Poppeli und Wattepusch dagegen bekamen zum Abendessen Brot, Milch und Brombeeren.

The Tale of Benjamin Bunny

Die Geschichte von Benjamin Purzel

One morning a little rabbit sat on a bank. He pricked his ears and listened to the trit-trot, trit-trot of a pony. A gig was coming along the road; it was driven by Mr McGregor, and beside him sat Mrs McGregor in her best bonnet.

As soon as they had passed, little Benjamin Bunny slid down into the road, and set off – with a hop, skip and a jump – to call upon his relations, who lived in the wood at the back of Mr McGregor's garden.

That wood was full of rabbit holes; and in the neatest sandiest hole of all, lived Benjamin's aunt and his cousins – Flopsy, Mopsy, Cottontail and Peter.

Old Mrs Rabbit was a widow; she earned her living by knitting rabbitwool mittens and muffetees (I once bought a pair at a bazaar). She also sold herbs, and rosemary tea, and

Eines Morgens hockte ein kleines Kaninchen auf einer Böschung. Es spitzte die Ohren und horchte auf das Tripptrapp, Tripptrapp eines Ponys. Ein offener Einspänner kam die Straße entlang. Er wurde von Herrn Gregerich kutschiert, und neben ihm saß Frau Gregerich, die ihren besten Hut aufhatte.

Sobald sie vorbeigefahren waren, rutschte der kleine Benjamin Purzel hinunter auf die Straße und machte sich mit einem Hopser, einem Sprung und einem Satz auf den Weg zu seinen Verwandten, die im Wald hinter Herrn Gregerichs Garten lebten.

In diesem Wald gab es viele Kaninchenbaue. Im saubersten und sandigsten Bau wohnten Benjamins Tante und seine Basen Hoppeli, Poppeli, Wattepusch und sein Vetter Peter.

Mutter Karnickel war Witwe. Sie verdiente ihren Unterhalt, indem sie Fäustlinge und Pulswärmer aus Kaninchenwolle strickte (ich habe einmal ein Paar auf einem Basar gekauft). Sie verkaufte auch Kräuter und

rabbit-tobacco (which is what *we* call lavender).

Little Benjamin did not very much want to see his Aunt. He came round the back of the fir-tree, and nearly tumbled upon the top of his Cousin Peter. Peter was sitting by himself. He looked poorly, and was dressed in a red cotton pocket-handkerchief.

"Peter," – said little Benjamin, in a whisper – "who has got your clothes?"

Peter replied – "The scarecrow in Mr McGregor's garden," and described how he had been chased about the garden, and had dropped his shoes and coat.

Little Benjamin sat down beside his cousin, and assured him that Mr McGregor had gone out in a gig, and Mrs McGregor also; and certainly for the day, because she was wearing her best bonnet.

Peter said he hoped that it would rain.

At this point, old Mrs Rabbit's voice was heard inside the rabbit hole, calling – "Cottontail! Cottontail! Fetch some more camomile!"

Peter said he thougt he might feel better if he went for a walk.

They went away hand in hand, and got upon the flat top of the wall at the bottom of the wood. From here they looked down into Mr McGregor's garden. Peter's coat and shoes were plainly to be seen upon the scarecrow, topped with an old tam-o-shanter of Mr McGregor's.

Little Benjamin said, "It spoils people's clothes to squeeze under a gate; the proper way to get in, is to climb down a pear tree."

Peter fell down head first; but it was of no

Rosmarintee und Kaninchentabak (wir nennen ihn Lavendel).

Der kleine Benjamin war nicht sehr darauf versessen, seiner Tante zu begegnen. Er kam hinten um die Kiefer herum und purzelte fast auf den Kopf seines Vetters Peter. Peter saß dort ganz allein. Er sah armselig aus, war nur mit einem roten baumwollenen Taschentuch bekleidet.

«Peter», sagte der kleine Benjamin flüsternd, «wer hat deine Anziehsachen?»

Peter antwortete: «Die Vogelscheuche im Garten von Herrn Gregerich.» Er berichtete, wie er im Garten herumgejagt worden war und Schuhe und Jacke verloren hatte.

Der kleine Benjamin setzte sich neben seinen Vetter und versicherte ihm, daß Herr Gregerich in einem offenen Einspänner ausgefahren sei und Frau Gregerich auch. Und bestimmt würden sie den ganzen Tag weg sein, denn sie hätte ihren besten Hut auf.

Peter sagte, daß er hoffe, es werde regnen.

In diesem Augenblick war die Stimme von Mutter Karnickel im Kaninchenbau zu hören. Sie rief: «Wattepusch! Wattepusch! Hol noch mehr Kamille, husch!»

Peter sagte, er glaube, vielleicht würde ein Spaziergang ihm guttun.

Sie gingen Hand in Hand davon und stiegen auf die flache Oberkante der Mauer am Waldrand. Von dort schauten sie hinunter in den Garten von Herrn Gregerich. Peters Jacke und Schuhe waren an der Vogelscheuche deutlich zu sehen. Zuoberst saß eine alte Pudelmütze von Herrn Gregerich.

Der kleine Benjamin sagte: «Es macht einem die Kleider kaputt, wenn man sich unter einem Gatter durchzwängt. Vernünftiger kommt man rein, wenn man an einem Birnbaum runterklettert.»

Peter fiel mit dem Kopf voran hinab. Doch es machte

consequence, as the bed below was newly raked and quite soft. It had been sown with lettuces. They left a great many odd little foot-marks all over the bed, especially little Benjamin, who was wearing clogs.

Little Benjamin said that the first thing to be done was to get back Peter's clothes, in order that they might be able to use the pocket-handkerchief.

They took them off the scarecrow. There had been rain during the night; there was water in the shoes, and the coat was somewhat shrunk. Benjamin tried on the tam-o-shanter, but it was too big for him.

Then he suggested that they should fill the pocket-handkerchief with onions, as a little present for his Aunt.

ihm nichts aus, weil das Beet drunten frisch geharkt und ganz weich war. Darin war Salat angesät worden. Sie hinterließen viele komische kleine Fußabdrücke übers ganze Beet verstreut, besonders der kleine Benjamin, der Holzpantoffeln trug.

Der kleine Benjamin sagte, daß es ihre erste Aufgabe sei, sich wieder Peters Anziehsachen zu verschaffen, damit sie das Taschentuch in Gebrauch nehmen könnten.

Sie holten die Sachen von der Vogelscheuche herunter. Über Nacht hatte es geregnet. In den Schuhen war Wasser, und die Jacke war etwas eingelaufen. Benjamin versuchte die Pudelmütze aufzusetzen, doch sie war ihm zu groß.

Dann schlug er vor, daß sie das Taschentuch mit Zwiebeln vollpacken sollten, als kleines Geschenk für seine Tante.

Peter did not seem to be enjoying himself; he kept hearing noises. Benjamin, on the contrary, was perfectly at home, and ate a lettuce leaf. He said that he was in the habit of coming to the garden with his father to get lettuces for their Sunday dinner. (The name of little Benjamin's papa was old Mr Benjamin Bunny.) The lettuces certainly were very fine.

Peter did not eat anything; he said he should like to go home. Presently he dropped half the onions.

Little Benjamin said that it was not possible to get back up the pear-tree, with a load of vegetables. He led the way boldly towards the other end of the garden. They went along a little walk on planks, under a sunny redbrick wall.

The mice sat on their door-steps cracking cherrystones, they winked at Peter Rabbit and little Benjamin Bunny.

Presently Peter let the pocket-handkerchief go again.

They got amongst flowerpots, and frames and tubs; Peter heard noises worse than ever, his eyes were as big as lolly-pops!

He was a step or two in front of his cousin, when he suddenly stopped. This is what those little rabbits saw round that corner! Little Ben-

Peter hatte anscheinend keinen so rechten Spaß. In einem fort hörte er Geräusche. Benjamin dagegen fühlte sich völlig wie zu Hause und aß ein Salatblatt. Er sagte, daß er meistens mit seinem Vater in den Garten komme, um Salat für das Sonntagsmittagessen zu holen. (Der Papa des kleinen Benjamin hieß Vater Benjamin Purzel). Der Salat war wirklich ausgezeichnet.

Peter aß gar nichts. Er sagte, er wolle lieber nach Hause gehen. Da fiel ihm die Hälfte der Zwiebeln aus der Tasche.

Der kleine Benjamin sagte, daß es unmöglich sei, mit einer Ladung Gemüse über den Birnbaum zurückzukehren. Kühn schlug er die Richtung zum anderen Ende des Gartens ein. Sie gingen auf einem kleinen Seitenweg aus Bohlen eine sonnenbeschienene rote Ziegelmauer entlang.

Die Mäuse saßen auf ihren Türschwellen und knackten Kirschkerne. Sie zwinkerten Peter Karnickel und dem kleinen Benjamin Purzel zu.

Da rutschte wieder das Taschentuch Peter aus der Hand.

Sie gingen zwischen Blumentöpfen, Frühbeeten und Bottichen. Peter hörte schlimmer denn je Geräusche. Seine Augen waren groß wie Dauerlutscher.

Er war einen oder zwei Schritte vor seinem Vetter, als er plötzlich stehenblieb. Was erblickten die beiden kleinen Kaninchen hinter der nächsten Ecke? Der

jamin took one look, and then, in half a minute less than no time, he hid himself and Peter and the onions underneath a large basket ...

The cat got up and stretched herself, and came and sniffed at the basket. Perhaps she liked the smell of onions! Anyway, she sat down upon the top of the basket. She sat there for *five hours*.

I cannot draw you a picture of Peter and Benjamin underneath the basket, because it was quite dark, and because the smell of onions was fearful; it made Peter Rabbit and little Benjamin cry.

The sun got round behind the wood, and it was quite late in the afternoon; but still the cat sat upon the basket.

At length there was a pitter-patter, pitter-patter, and some bits of mortar fell from the wall above.

The cat looked up und saw old Mr Benjamin Bunny prancing along the top of the wall of the upper terrace. He was smoking a pipe of rabbit-tobacco, and had a little switch in his hand. He was looking for his son.

Old Mr Bunny had no opinion whatever of cats. He took a tremendous jump off the top of the wall on to the top of the cat, and cuffed it off the basket, and kicked it into the greenhouse, scratching off a handful of fur. The cat was too much surprised to scratch back.

When old Mr Bunny had driven the cat into the greenhouse, he locked the door.

Then he came back to the basket and took out his son Benjamin by the ears, and whipped him with the little switch.

kleine Benjamin schaute nur einmal hin und dann, in null Komma nichts, versteckte er sich und Peter und die Zwiebeln unter einem großen Korb.

Die Katze erhob sich und reckte sich, kam heran und schnupperte an dem Korb. Vielleicht mochte sie den Geruch von Zwiebeln. Jedenfalls ließ sie sich oben auf dem Korb nieder. Sie blieb da fünf Stunden lang sitzen.

Ich kann euch kein Bild zeichnen, wie Peter und Benjamin unter dem Korb sitzen, weil es ganz dunkel und der Zwiebelgeruch entsetzlich war. Er brachte Peter Karnickel und den kleinen Benjamin Purzel zum Weinen.

Die Sonne machte ihre Runde um den Wald herum. Es wurde Spätnachmittag. Und die Katze saß noch immer auf dem Korb.

Schließlich hörte man ein Trippel-Trappel, Trippel-Trappel, und kleine Mörtelstücke fielen von der Mauer herab.

Die Katze schaute hoch und sah Vater Benjamin Purzel auf der Mauer der oberen Terrasse entlangstolzieren. Er schmauchte eine Pfeife Kaninchentabak und trug eine kleine Rute in der Hand. Er war auf der Suche nach seinem Sohn.

Vater Purzel hatte nicht den geringsten Respekt vor Katzen. Er machte einen gewaltigen Satz von der Oberkante der Mauer auf die Katze hinunter, knuffte sie vom Korb weg und schubste sie ins Treibhaus, wobei er eine Handvoll von ihrem Fell auskratzte. Die Katze war viel zu überrascht, um zurückzukratzen.

Nachdem Vater Purzel die Katze ins Treibhaus gejagt hatte, schloß er die Tür hinter ihr ab.

Dann kam er wieder zum Korb und zog seinen Sohn Benjamin an den Ohren hervor und versohlte ihn mit der kleinen Rute.

Then he took out his nephew Peter.

Then he took out the handkerchief of onions, and marched out of the garden.

When Mr McGregor returned about half an hour later, he observed several things which perplexed him. It looked as though some person had been walking all over the garden in a pair of clogs – only the footmarks were too ridiculously little! Also he could not understand how the cat could have managed to shut herself up *inside* the green-house, locking the door upon the *outside*.

When Peter got home, his mother forgave him, because she was so glad to see that he had found his shoes and coat. Cottontail and Peter folded up the pocket-handkerchief, and old Mrs Rabbit strung up the onions and hung them from the kitchen ceiling, with the bunches of herbs and the rabbit-tobacco.

Dann zog er seinen Neffen Peter hervor.

Dann zog er das Taschentuch mit den Zwiebeln hervor und marschierte aus dem Garten.

Als Herr Gregerich ungefähr eine halbe Stunde später nach Hause kam, bemerkte er manches, was ihn verwunderte. Es sah so aus, als ob irgendjemand kreuz und quer im ganzen Garten herumgelaufen war, und zwar in Holzpantoffeln – nur waren die Fußstapfen gar so lächerlich klein. Auch konnte er sich nicht erklären, wie die Katze es fertiggebracht hatte, sich selber innen im Treibhaus einzusperren und die Tür von außen zu verschließen.

Als Peter nach Hause kam, verzieh ihm seine Mutter, weil sie froh war zu sehen, daß er seine Schuhe und seine Jacke gefunden hatte. Wattepusch und Peter falteten das Taschentuch zusammen, und Mutter Karnickel zog die Zwiebeln auf eine Schnur und hängte sie an die Küchendecke, wo die Kräuterbüschel und der Kaninchentabak hingen.

The Tale of Mrs Tiggy-Winkle

Die Geschichte von Frau Pieke-Schnack

Once upon a time there was a little girl called Lucie, who lived at a farm called Little-town. She was a good little girl – only she was always losing her pocket-handkerchiefs!

One day little Lucie came into the farm-yard crying – oh, she did cry so! "I've lost my pocket-handkin! Three handkins and a pinny! Have *you* seen them, Tabby Kitten?"

The kitten went on washing her white paws; so Lucie asked a speckled hen – "Sally Henny-penny, have *you* found three pocket-hand-kins?"

But the speckled hen ran into a barn, cluck-ing – "I go barefoot, barefoot, barefoot!"

And then Lucie asked Cook Robin sitting on a twig. Cock Robin looked sideways at Lucie

Es war einmal ein kleine Mädchen, das hieß Lucie. Es lebte auf einem Bauernhof, der Kleinflecken hieß. Es war ein liebes kleines Mädchen, nur verlor es ständig seine Taschentücher.

Eines Tages kam die kleine Lucie weinend in den Wirtschaftshof – oh, und wie sie weinte! «Ich habe mein Taschentuch verloren. Drei Taschentücher und ein Schürzchen! Hast du sie gesehen, Tigerkätzchen?»

Das Kätzchen putzte nur unentwegt seine weißen Pfoten. Da fragte Lucie eine gesprenkelte Henne: «Sara Hennchen-Fiederchen, hast du drei Taschentücher gesehen?»

Doch die gesprenkelte Henne lief in eine Scheune und gackerte: «Ich gehe barfuß, barfuß, barfuß!»

Da fragte Lucie Hähnchen Rotkehl, der auf einem Zweig saß. Hähnchen Rotkehl blickte mit seinem

with his bright black eye, and he flew over a
stile and away.

Lucie climbed upon the stile and looked up at
the hill behind Little-town – a hill that goes
up-up-into the clouds as though it had no top!
And a great way up the hillside she thought
she saw some white things spread upon the
grass.

Lucie scrambled up the hill as fast as her
stout legs would carry her; she ran along a
steep path-way – up and up – until Little-town
was right away down below – she could have
dropped a pebble down the chimney!

Presently she came to a spring, bubbling out
from the hill-side. Someone had stood a tin can
upon a stone to catch the water – but the water
was already running over, for the can was no
bigger than an egg-cup! And where the sand
upon the path was wet – there were footmarks
of a *very* small person.

Lucie ran on, and on.

The path ended under a big rock. The grass
was short and green, and there were clothes-
props cut from bracken stems, with lines of
plaited rushes, and a heap of tiny clothes pins
– but no pocket-handkerchiefs!

But there was something else – a door!
straight into the hill; and inside it someone
was singing –

"Lily-white and clean, oh!
With little frills between, oh!
Smooth and hot – red rusty spot
Never here be seen, oh!"

Lucie knocked – once – twice, and inter-
rupted the song. A little frightened voice called
out "Who's that?"

blanken schwarzen Auge schräg auf Lucie und flog
über einen Zauntritt davon.

Lucie stieg auf den Zauntritt und sah hinauf zu dem
Hügel hinter Kleinflecken – einem Hügel, der hoch
aufragte, bis in die Wolken, als hätte er gar keinen
Gipfel. Und ein großes Stück hügelaufwärts glaubte
sie einige weiße Sachen auf dem Gras ausgebreitet
zu sehen.

Lucie kletterte den Hügel hinauf, so schnell ihre
runden Beine sie trugen. Sie lief auf einem steilen
Pfad, höher und höher, bis Kleinflecken genau unter
ihr lag. Sie hätte einen Kieselstein in den Schornstein
werfen können.

Da kam sie zu einer Quelle, die aus dem Hügel
sprudelte. Jemand hatte eine Blechbüchse auf einen
Stein gestellt, um das Wasser aufzufangen. Doch das
Wasser lief schon längst über, denn die Büchse war
nicht größer als ein Eierbecher. Wo der Sand auf dem
Weg naß war, gab es Fußabdrücke von einer sehr
kleinen Person.

Lucie lief weiter und weiter.

Der Weg endete unter einem großen Felsen. Das
Gras war kurz und grün, und da standen Wäsche-
pfosten, die aus Stielen des Adlerfarns geschnitten
waren, mit Wäscheleinen aus geflochtenen Binsen.
Auch gab es ganz viele winzige Wäscheklammern –
doch keine Taschentücher!

Aber es gab etwas anderes: eine Tür direkt in den
Berg hinein. Und dahinter sang jemand:

> «Lilienweiß und rein, oh!
> Mit kleinen Rüschen drein, oh!
> Glatt und heiß – ein Rostfleck
> wird hier niemals sein, oh!»

Lucie klopfte einmal, zweimal, und unterbrach damit das Lied. Eine kleine erschrockene Stimme rief:
«Wer ist da?»

Lucie opened the door: and what do you think there was inside the hill? – a nice clean kitchen with a flagged floor and wooden beams – just like any other farm kitchen. Only the ceiling was so low that Lucie's head nearly touched it; and the pots and pans were small, and so was everything there.

There was a nice hot singey smell; and at the table, with an iron in her hand stood a very stout short person staring anxiously at Lucie. Her print gown was tucked up, and she was wearing a large apron over her striped petticoat. Her little black nose went sniffle, sniffle, snuffle, and her eyes went twinkle, twinkle; and underneath her cap – where Lucie had yellow curls – that little person had *Prickles*!

"Who are you?" said Lucie. "Have you seen my pocket-handkins?"

The little person made a bob-curtsey – "Oh, yes, if you please'm; my name is Mrs Tiggy-winkle; oh, yes if you please'm, I'm an excel-

Lucie öffnete die Tür. Und was glaubst du war in dem Berg? Eine hübsche saubere Küche mit einem gepflasterten Fußboden und einer Bohlendecke – genau wie jede andere Küche in einem Bauernhof. Nur war die Decke so niedrig, daß Lucies Kopf sie fast berührte. Die Töpfe und Pfannen waren klein, und klein war alles, was es dort gab.

Es herrschte ein wohlig dämpfiger Geruch. Am Tisch stand, mit einem Bügeleisen in der Hand, eine sehr rundliche kleine Person, die Lucie ängstlich anstarrte. Ihr Kattunkleid war hochgerafft, und über ihrem gestreiften Unterrock trug sie eine große Schürze. Sie schnüffelte und schnupperte mit ihrer kleinen schwarzen Nase und blinzelte und zwinkerte mit den Augen. Und unter ihrer Haube, dort, wo Lucie gelbe Locken hatte, trug die kleine Person Stacheln!

«Wer bist du?» fragte Lucie. «Hast du meine Taschentücher gesehen?»

Die kleine Person machte einen höflichen Knicks. «Oh, ja, mit Verlaub! Ich bin Frau Pieke-Schnack. Oh, ja, mit Verlaub, ich bin eine ausgezeichnete Wäsche-

lent clear-starcher!" And she took something out of a clothes-basket, and spread it on the ironing-blanket.

"What's that thing?" said Lucie – "That's not my pocket-handkin?"

"Oh no, if you please'm; that's a little scarlet waist-coat belonging to Cock Robin!" And she ironed it and folded it, and put it on one side.

Then she took something else off a clothes-horse –

"That isn't my pinny?" said Lucie.

"Oh no, if you please'm; that's a damask table-cloth belonging to Jenny Wren; look how it's stained with currant wine! It's very bad to wash!" said Mrs Tiggy-winkle.

Mrs Tiggy-winkle's nose went sniffle, sniffle, snuffle, and her eyes went twinkle, twinkle; and she fetched another hot iron from the fire.

"There's one of my pocket-handkins!" cried Lucie – "And there's my pinny!"

Mrs Tiggy-winkle ironed it, and goffered it, and shook out the frills.

"Oh that *is* lovely!" said Lucie. "And what are those long yellow things with fingers like gloves?"

"Oh, that's a pair of stockings belonging to Sally Henny-penny – look how she's worn the heels out with scratching in the yard! She'll very soon go barefoot!" said Mrs Tiggy-winkle.

"Why, there's another handkersniff – but it isn't mine; it's red?"

"Oh no, if you please'm; that one belongs to old Mrs Rabbit; and it *did* so smell of onions! I've had to wash it separately, I can't get out the smell."

stärkerin.» Und sie nahm etwas aus dem Wäschekorb und breitete es auf dem Bügeltuch aus.

«Was ist das?» fragte Lucie. «Ist das nicht mein Taschentuch?»

«Oh, nein, mit Verlaub! Das ist ein scharlachrotes Wämschen, das Hähnchen Rotkehl gehört.» Und sie bügelte es, faltete es zusammen und legte es zur Seite.

Dann nahm sie etwas anderes von einem Trockengestell.

«Ist das nicht mein Schürzchen?» sagte Lucie.

«Oh, nein, mit Verlaub! Das ist ein Damasttischtuch, das Hanni Brehm gehört. Schau nur, wie es mit Johannisbeerwein verfleckt ist! Es läßt sich sehr schwer auswaschen», sagte Frau Pieke-Schnack.

Frau Pieke-Schnack schnüffelte und schnupperte mit der Nase und blinzelte und zwinkerte mit den Augen. Sie holte ein frisches heißes Eisen vom Feuer.

«Aber das ist ein Taschentuch von mir!» rief Lucie. «Und da ist mein Schürzchen!»

Frau Pieke-Schnack bügelte und fältelte sie und schüttelte die Rüschen aus.

«Oh, das ist wunderschön!» sagte Lucie. «Und was sind das für lange gelbe Dinger mit Fingern wie bei Handschuhen?»

«Oh, das sind ein Paar Strümpfe, die Sara Hennchen-Fiederchen gehören. Schau nur, wie sie die Fersen durchgescheuert hat mit dem vielen Kratzen im Hof! Sie wird bald barfuß gehen müssen», sagte Frau Pieke-Schnack.

«Da, da ist noch ein Schnupftuch! Doch es gehört nicht mir. Es ist rot.»

«Oh, nein, mit Verlaub! Es gehört Mutter Karnickel. Und wie es nach Zwiebeln gerochen hat! Ich mußte es getrennt waschen, und doch bekomme ich den Geruch nicht raus.»

"There's another one of mine," said Lucie. "What are those funny little white things?"

"That's a pair of mittens belonging to Tabby Kitten; I only have to iron them; she washes them herself."

"There's my last pocket-handkin!" said Lucie. "And what are you dipping into the basin of starch?"

"They're little dicky shirt-fronts belonging to Tom Titmouse – most terrible particular!" said Mrs Tiggy-winkle. "Now I've finished my ironing; I'm going to air some clothes."

"What are these dear soft fluffy things?" said Lucie.

"Oh those are wolly coats belonging to the little lambs at Skelghyl."

"Will their jackets take off?" asked Lucie.

"Oh yes, if you please'm; look at the sheep-mark on the shoulder. And here's one marked

«Da ist noch eins von meinen», sagte Lucie. «Aber was sind das dort für lustige kleine weiße Dinger?»

«Das sind ein Paar Fäustlinge, die Tigerkätzchen gehören. Ich muß sie nur bügeln. Das Waschen besorgt sie selber.»

«Hier ist mein letztes Taschentuch!» sagte Lucie. «Aber was tauchst du in die Schüssel, wo die Stärke drin ist?»

«Es sind Krägelchen, die Michi Meise gehören. Er ist schrecklich eigen», sagte Frau Pieke-Schnack. «Jetzt bin ich mit meiner Bügelwäsche fertig. Ich will noch einige Kleider zum Trocknen aufhängen.»

«Was sind diese allerliebsten weichen flaumigen Sachen?» fragte Lucie.

«Oh, das sind wollene Jacken, die den kleinen Lämmern auf dem Hardthof gehören.»

«Kann man die Jacken ausziehen?» fragte Lucie.

«Oh, ja, mit Verlaub! Schau dir doch das Zeichen auf der Schulter an. Hier ist eines mit dem Zeichen von

for Gatesgarth, and three that come from Little-town. They're *always* marked at washing!" said Mrs Tiggy-winkle.

And she hung up all sorts and sizes of clothes – small brown coats of mice; and one velvety black mole-skin waist-coat; and a red tail-coat with no tail belonging to Squirrel Nutkin; and a very much shrunk blue jacket belonging to Peter Rabbit; and a petticoat, not marked, that had gone lost in the washing – and at last the basket was empty!

Then Mrs Tiggy-winkle made tea – a cup for herself and a cup for Lucie. They sat before the fire on a bench and looked sideways at one another. Mrs Tiggy-winkle's hand, holding the tea-cup, was very very brown, and very very wrinkly with the soap-suds; and all through her gown and her cap, there were *hair-pins* sticking wrong end out; so that Lucie didn't like to sit too near her.

Klosterpforta, und drei stammen von Kleinflecken. Zur Wäsche werden sie immer gezeichnet», sagte Frau Pieke-Schnack.

Sie hängte alle möglichen Sorten und Größen von Kleidern auf: Kleine braune Mäntel von Mäusen und eine samtene schwarze Fellweste vom Maulwurf. Einen roten Frack ohne Frackschöße, der Eichkater Nüßlein gehörte, und eine ziemlich eingelaufene blaue Jacke, die von Peter Karnickel stammte. Und einen Unterrock ohne Zeichen! Das war beim Waschen verlorengegangen. Schließlich war der Wäschekorb leer.

Nun machte Frau Pieke-Schnack Tee. Eine Tasse für sich selber und eine für Lucie. Sie saßen auf einer Bank vor dem Kamin und wandten sich schräg einander zu. Frau Pieke-Schnacks Hand, mit der sie die Teetasse hielt, war sehr sehr braun und sehr sehr runzlig von der vielen Seifenlauge. Durch alle ihre Kleider und durch ihre Haube staken Haarnadeln mit dem falschen Ende nach draußen, so daß Lucie nicht allzu nah bei ihr sitzen mochte.

When they had finished tea, they tied up the clothes in bundles; and Lucie's pocket-handkerchiefs were folded up inside her clean pinny, and fastened with a silver safety-pin. And then they made up the fire with turf, and came out and locked the door, and hid the key under the door-sill.

Then away down the hill trotted Lucie and Mrs Tiggy-winkle with the bundles of clothes! All the way down the path little animals came out of the fern to meet them; the very first that they met were Peter Rabbit and Benjamin Bunny! And she gave them their nice clean clothes; and all the little animals and birds were so very much obliged to dear Mrs Tiggy-winkle.

So that at the bottom of the hill when they came to the stile, there was nothing left to carry except Lucie's one little bundle. Lucie scrambled up the stile with the bundle in her hand; and then she turned to say Good-night,

Als sie Tee getrunken hatten, banden sie die Kleider zu Bündeln. Lucies Taschentücher wurden zusammengefaltet in ihr sauberes Schürzchen gelegt und mit einer silbernen Sicherheitsnadel befestigt. Dann versorgten sie das Feuer mit Torf, traten ins Freie, schlossen die Tür ab und versteckten den Schlüssel unter der Türschwelle.

Nun trotteten Lucie und Frau Pieke-Schnack mit den Kleiderbündeln den Abhang hinunter. Überall auf ihrem Hinunterweg traten kleine Tiere aus dem Farnkraut hervor, um sie zu begrüßen. Die allerersten, die ihnen begegneten, waren Peter Karnickel und Benjamin Purzel. Frau Pieke-Schnack gab ihnen ihre schönen sauberen Kleider, und all die kleinen Tiere und die Vögel waren der lieben Frau Pieke-Schnack überaus dankbar.

So hatten sie am Fuß des Hügels, als sie den Zauntritt erreichten, nichts mehr zu tragen als Lucies kleines Wäschebündel. Lucie kletterte mit dem Bündel in der Hand auf den Zauntritt, dann wandte sie sich um und wollte «Gute Nacht» sagen und der Waschfrau danken.

and to thank the washer-woman – But what a *very* odd thing! Mrs Tiggy-winkle had not waited either for thanks or for the washing bill!

She was running running running up the hill – and where was her white frilled cap? and her shawl? and her gown – and her petticoat? And *how* small she had grown – and *how* brown – and covered with *Prickles*!

Why! Mrs Tiggy-winkle was nothing but a *Hedgehog*!

(Now some people say that little Lucie had been asleep upon the stile – but then how could she have found three clean pocket-handkins and a pinny, pinned with a silver safety-pin?

And besides – *I* have seen that door into the back of the hill called Cat Bells – and besides *I* am very well acquainted with dear Mrs Tiggy-winkle!)

Doch, wie höchst sonderbar! Frau Pieke-Schnack hatte weder den Dank noch die Bezahlung der Wäsche abgewartet.

Sie lief, lief und lief den Hang hinauf – wo waren nur ihre weiße Rüschenhaube und ihr Schultertuch und ihr Kleid und ihr Unterrock? Und wie klein sie geworden war und wie braun und ganz mit Stacheln bedeckt!

Nun ja! Frau Pieke-Schnack war nichts anderes als ein Igel.

(Einige Leute meinen jetzt, daß die kleine Lucie auf dem Zauntritt eingeschlafen war. Doch wie hätte sie dann drei saubere Taschentücher und ein Schürzchen, die mit einer silbernen Sicherheitsnadel zusammengesteckt waren, finden können?

Außerdem habe ich die besagte Tür am Hang des Hügels, der Katzenschelle heißt, selber gesehen, und außerdem sind die liebe Frau Pieke-Schnack und ich sehr gute Bekannte.)

The Tale of the Flopsy Bunnies

Die Geschichte von den Hoppeli Purzels

It is said that the effect of eating too much lettuce is "soporific". *I* have never felt sleepy after
eating lettuces; but then *I* am not a rabbit.
They certainly had a very soporific effect upon the Flopsy Bunnies!

When Benjamin Bunny grew up, he married
his Cousin Flopsy. They had a large family,
and they were very improvident and cheerful.
I do not remember the separate names of their
children; they were generally called the
"Flopsy Bunnies".

As there was not always quite enough to
eat – Benjamin used to borrow cabbages from
Flopsy's brother, Peter Rabbit, who kept a
nursery garden. Sometimes Peter Rabbit had
no cabbages to spare. When this happened,
the Flopsy Bunnies went across the field to a
rubbish heap, in the ditch outside Mr McGregor's garden.

Mr McGregor's rubbish heap was a mixture.
There were jam pots and paper bags, and

Zu viel Salat hat angeblich eine einschläfernde Wirkung. Ich für mein Teil war, wenn ich Salat gegessen habe, nie schläfrig. Aber ich bin ja auch kein Kaninchen. Doch die einschläfernde Wirkung von Salat auf die Hoppeli Purzels war unbestreitbar.

Als Benjamin Purzel alt genug war, heiratete er seine Base Hoppeli. Sie wurden eine große Familie, und sie waren sehr unbekümmert und vergnügt. Ich kann mich an die einzelnen Namen ihrer Kinder nicht erinnern. Sie wurden überall die «Hoppeli Purzels» genannt.

Da sie nicht immer genug zu essen hatten, nahm Vater Benjamin machmal etwas Kohl von Hoppelis Bruder zu leihen, von Peter Karnickel, der einen Gemüsegarten hatte. Aber manchmal hatte Peter Karnickel keinen Kohl übrig. Wenn das der Fall war, zogen die Hoppeli Purzels über das Feld zu einem Abfallhaufen im Graben außerhalb von Herrn Gregerichs Garten.

Der Abfallhaufen von Herrn Gregerich war ein Mischmasch. Da lagen Marmeladengläser und Pa-

mountains of chopped grass from the mowing machine (which always tasted oily), and some rotten vegetable marrows and an old boot or two.

One day – oh joy! – there were a quantity of overgrown lettuces, which had "shot" into flower. The Flopsy Bunnies simply stuffed lettuces. By degrees, one after another, they were overcome with slumber, and lay down in the mown grass.

Benjamin was not so much overcome as his children. Before going to sleep he was sufficiently wide awake to put a paper bag over his head to keep off the flies.

The little Flopsy Bunnies slept delightfully in the warm sun. From the lawn beyond the garden came the distant clacketty sound of the mowing machine. The blue-bottles buzzed about the wall, and a little old mouse picked over the rubbish among the jam pots. (I can tell you her name, she was called Thomasina Tittlemouse, a woodmouse with a long tail.) She rustled across the paper bag, and awakened Benjamin Bunny.

The mouse apologized profusely, and said that she knew Peter Rabbit.

While she and Benjamin were talking, close under the wall, they heard a heavy tread above their heads; and suddenly Mr McGregor emptied out a sackful of lawn mowings right upon the top of the sleeping Flopsy Bunnies! Benjamin shrank down under his paper bag. The mouse hid in a jam pot.

The little rabbits smiled sweetly in their sleep under the shower of grass; they did not awake because the lettuces had been so sopori-

träumten, daß ihre Mutter Hoppeli sie in ein Heubett packte.

Nachdem Herr Gregerich seinen Sack geleert hatte, schaute er hinunter. Er sah ein paar komische kleine braune Ohrspitzen aus dem gemähten Gras gucken. Er starrte sie eine Zeitlang an.

Da ließ sich eine Fliege auf eine Ohrspitze nieder, und die bewegte sich.

Herr Gregerich stieg hinunter auf den Abfallhaufen. «Eins, zwei, drei, vier! fünf! sechs kleine Kaninchen!» sagte er, als er sie eins ums andere in seinen Sack steckte.

Die Hoppeli Purzels meinten im Traum, daß ihre Mutter sie im Bett umdrehte. Sie rührten sich ein wenig in ihrem Schlaf, wachten aber immer noch nicht auf.

Herr Gregerich band den Sack zu und ließ ihn auf der Mauer liegen. Er ging, um den Rasenmäher aufzuräumen.

While he was gone, Mrs Flopsy Bunny (who had remained at home) came across the field. She looked suspiciously at the sack and wondered where everybody was?

Then the mouse came out of her jam pot, and Benjamin took the paper bag off his head, and they told the doleful tale.

Benjamin and Flopsy were in despair, they could not undo the string. But Mrs Tittlemouse was a resourceful person. She nibbled a hole in the bottom corner of the sack. The little rabbits were pulled out and pinched to wake them.

Their parents stuffed the empty sack with three rotten vegetable marrows, an old blacking-brush and two decayed turnips.

Then they all hid under a bush and watched for Mr McGregor.

Mr McGregor came back and picked up the sack, and carried it off. He carried it hanging down, as if it were rather heavy.

The Flopsy Bunnies followed at a safe dis-

Während er weg war, kam Frau Hoppeli Purzel (die zu Hause geblieben war) über das Feld. Sie blickte argwöhnisch auf den Sack und fragte sich, wo sie alle waren.

Da kam die Maus aus ihrem Marmeladenglas, und Benjamin nahm die Papiertüte vom Kopf, und sie erzählten die traurige Geschichte.

Benjamin und Hoppeli waren verzweifelt. Sie konnten die Schnur nicht aufknoten. Doch Thomasina Pünktchen war eine findige Person. Sie knabberte ein Loch in den unteren Zipfel des Sackes. Die kleinen Kaninchen wurden herausgezogen und gekniffen, damit sie aufwachten.

Ihre Eltern stopften drei faulige Eierkürbisse, eine alte Wichsbürste und zwei verrottete Steckrüben in den leeren Sack.

Dann versteckten sie sich alle unter einem Busch und warteten auf Herrn Gregerich.

Herr Gregerich kam zurück, hob den Sack auf und trug ihn davon. Er hing schwer an seiner Hand, als hätte er ein ziemliches Gewicht.

Die Hoppeli Purzels folgten in sicherer Entfernung.

tance. They watched him go into his house. And then they crept up to the window to listen.

Mr McGregor threw down the sack on the stone floor in a way that would have been extremely painful to the Flopsy Bunnies, if they had happened to have been inside it.

They could hear him drag his chair on the flags, and chuckle – "One, two, three, four, five, six leetle rabbits!" said Mr McGregor.

"Eh? What's that? What have they been spoiling now?" inquired Mrs McGregor.

"One, two, three, four, five, six leetle fat rabbits!" repeated Mr McGregor, counting on his fingers – "one, two, three –"

"Don't you be silly; what do you mean, you silly old man?"

"In the sack! One, two, three, four, five, six!" replied Mr McGregor.

(The youngest Flopsy Bunny got upon the window-sill.)

Sie sahen, wie er in sein Haus hineinging. Dann krochen sie ans Fenster, um zu lauschen.

Herr Gregerich ließ den Sack in einer Weise auf den Steinboden fallen, daß es für die Hoppeli Purzels höchst schmerzhaft gewesen wäre, wenn sie sich darin befunden hätten.

Sie konnten hören, wie er seinen Stuhl über die Steinfliesen zog und gluckste. «Eins, zwei, drei, vier, fünf, sechs kleine Kaninchen!» sagte Herr Gregerich.

«Wie? Was ist das? Was haben sie diesmal geplündert?» fragte Frau Gregerich.

«Eins, zwei, drei, vier, fünf, sechs fette kleine Kaninchen!» wiederholte Herr Gregerich und zählte sie an seinen Fingern ab, «eins, zwei, drei ...»

«Red' keinen Unsinn! Was meinst du damit, du närrischer alter Mann?»

«Hier im Sack! Eins, zwei, drei, vier, fünf, sechs!» antwortete Herr Gregerich.

(Das jüngste Hoppeli Purzel kletterte aufs Fensterbrett.)

Mrs McGregor took hold of the sack and felt it. She said she could feel six, but they must be *old* rabbits, because they were so hard and all different shapes.

"Not fit to eat; but the skins will do fine to line my old cloak."

"Line your old cloak?" shouted Mr Mc Gregor – I shall sell them and buy myself baccy!"

"Rabbit tobacco! I shall skin them and cut off their heads."

Mrs McGregor untied the sack and put her hand inside. When she felt the vegetables she became very very angry. She said that Mr McGregor had "done it a purpose".

And Mr McGregor was very angry too. One of the rotten marrows came flying through the kitchen window, and hit the youngest Flopsy Bunny. It was rather hurt. Then Benjamin and Flopsy thought that it was time to go home.

So Mr McGregor did not get his tobacco, and Mrs McGregor did not get her rabbit skins.

But next Christmas Thomasina Tittlemouse got a present of enough rabbit-wool to make herself a cloak and a hood, and a handsome muff and a pair of warm mittens.

Frau Gregerich packte den Sack und tastete ihn ab. Sie sagte, daß sie sechs fühlen könne, doch es müßten alte Kaninchen sein, weil sie sich so fest anfaßten, und alle seien unterschiedlich groß.

«Nichts zum Essen! Doch die Felle kann ich für einen Saum an meinem alten Mantel gebrauchen.»

«Einen Saum für deinen alten Mantel?» rief Herr Gregerich. «Ich werde sie zu Geld machen und mir davon Tabak kaufen.»

«Kaninchentabak! Ich werde ihnen das Fell über die Ohren ziehen und ihnen die Köpfe abschneiden.»

Frau Gregerich band den Sack auf und steckte die Hand hinein. Als sie das Gemüse fühlte, wurde sie sehr, sehr ärgerlich. Sie meinte, daß Herr Gregerich es mit Absicht getan habe.

Herr Gregerich wurde auch sehr ärgerlich. Ein fauliger Eierkürbis flog durchs Küchenfenster und traf das jüngste Hoppeli Purzel. Das tat ihm ziemlich weh. Da dachten Benjamin und Hoppeli, daß es an der Zeit sei heimzugehen.

So bekam Herr Gregerich keinen Tabak und Frau Gregerich keine Kaninchenfelle.

Aber zum nächsten Weihnachtsfest bekam Thomasina Pünktchen als Geschenk genug Kaninchenwolle, um sich einen Mantel, eine Kapuze, einen schönen Muff und ein paar warme Fäustlinge zu machen.

The Tale of Mr Tod

Die Geschichte von Junker Voss

I have made many books about well-behaved people. Now, for a change, I am going to make a story about two disagreeable people, called Tommy Brock and Mr Tod.

Nobody could call Mr Tod "nice". The rabbits could not bear him; they could smell him half a mile off. He was of a wandering habit and he had foxey whiskers; they never knew where he would be next.

One day he was living in a stick-house in the coppice, causing terror to the family of old Mr Benjamin Bouncer. Next day he moved into a pollard willow near the lake, frightening the wild ducks and the water rats. In winter and early spring he might generally be found in an earth amongst the rocks at the top of Bull Banks, under Oatmeal Crag.

He had half a dozen houses, but he was seldom at home.

The houses were not always empty when Mr Tod moved *out*; because sometimes Tommy Brock moved *in*; (without asking leave).

Tommy Brock was a short bristly fat waddling person with a grin; he grinned all over his face. He was not nice in his habits. He ate wasp nests and frogs and worms; and he waddled about by moonlight, digging things up.

His clothes were very dirty; and as he slept in the day-time, he always went to bed in his boots. And the bed which he went to bed in, was generally Mr Tod's.

Now Tommy Brock did occasionally eat rabbit-pie; but it was only very little young ones occasionally, when other food was really scarce.

Ich habe viele Bücher über manierliche Leute geschrieben. Jetzt werde ich zur Abwechslung eine Geschichte über zwei unerfreuliche Gestalten schreiben. Sie hießen Meister Gräving und Junker Voss.

Niemand fand Junker Voss «nett». Die Kaninchen konnten ihn nicht ausstehen. Sie witterten ihn schon eine halbe Meile weit weg. Er hatte die Gewohnheit herumzustreunen und trug einen rotbraunen Bart. Sie wußten nie, wo er als nächstes auftauchen würde.

Den einen Tag wohnte er in einem Haus aus Reisig im Gehölz und sorgte für Bestürzung in der Familie von Vater Purzel. Am nächsten Tag zog er um in eine gestutzte Weide dicht am See und versetzte die Wildenten und Wasserratten in Furcht und Schrecken. Im Winter und Vorfrühling konnte man ihn meistens in einem Bau zwischen den Felsen auf dem Ochsenkopf unterm Haberbuckel antreffen.

Er hatte ein halbes Dutzend Behausungen, doch er war selten daheim.

Diese Behausungen blieben nicht immer unbewohnt, wenn Junker Voss auszog, weil manchmal Meister Gräving einzog, ohne Erlaubnis.

Meister Gräving war ein kurzes borstiges fettes watschelndes Wesen, ein grinsendes Wesen. Er grinste übers ganze Gesicht. Er hatte keine feinen Gewohnheiten. Er aß Wespennester und Frösche und Würmer. Und er watschelte bei Mondschein umher und grub alles mögliche aus.

Seine Kleidung war sehr schmutzig, und da er tagsüber schlief, ging er immer mit Stiefeln zu Bett. Das Bett, in das er zu Bett ging, gehörte meistens Junker Voss.

Manchmal aß Meister Gräving auch Kaninchenpastete, doch nur aus sehr kleinen Jungkaninchen, manchmal, wenn andere Nahrung wirklich knapp war.

He was friendly with old Mr Bouncer; they agreed in disliking the wicked otters and Mr Tod; they often talked over that painful subject.

Old Mr Bouncer was stricken in years. He sat in the spring sunshine outside the burrow, in a muffler; smoking a pipe of rabbit tobacco. He lived with his son Benjamin Bunny and his daughter-in-law Flopsy, who had a young family. Old Mr Bouncer was in charge of the family the afternoon, because Benjamin and Flopsy had gone out.

The little rabbit-babies were just old enough to open their blue eyes and kick. They lay in a fluffy bed of rabbit wool and hay, in a shallow burrow, separate from the main rabbit hole. To tell the truth – old Mr Bouncer had forgotten them. He sat in the sun, and conversed cordially with Tommy Brock, who was passing through the wood with a sack and a little spud which he used for digging, and some mole traps. He complained bitterly about the scar-

Meister Gräving und Vater Purzel standen freundschaftlich zueinander. Sie waren sich einig, daß sie
die unverschämten Ottern und Junker Voss nicht
mochten. Sie sprachen oft über dieses leidige Thema.

Vater Purzel war schon hochbetagt. Er saß, in einen
Schal gehüllt, in der Frühlingssonne vor dem Bau und
schmauchte ein Pfeifchen Kaninchentabak. Er lebte bei
seinem Sohn Benjamin Purzel und seiner Schwieger-
tochter Hoppeli, die eine Schar Kinder hatten. Vater
Purzel war diesen Nachmittag für die Kleinen verant-
wortlich, weil Benjamin und Hoppeli ausgegangen
waren.

Die kleinen Kaninchenkinder waren gerade alt genug, daß sie ihre blauen Augen öffnen und strampeln
konnten. Sie lagen auf einem flaumigen Bett aus
Kaninchenwolle und Heu in einer niedrigen Höhle,
abgetrennt vom Hauptbau. Um die Wahrheit zu sagen:
Vater Purzel hatte sie vergessen. Er saß in der Sonne
und unterhielt sich freundschaftlich mit Meister Gräving, der mit einem Sack und einem kleinen Jätspaten,
den er zum Graben benutzte, und ein paar Maulwurfs-
fallen durch den Wald gezogen kam. Er beklagte sich

city of pheasants' eggs, and accused Mr Tod of poaching them. And the otters had cleared off all the frogs while he was asleep in winter – "I have not had a good square meal for a fortnight, I am living on pig-nuts. I shall have to turn vegetarian and eat my own tail!" said Tommy Brock.

It was not much of a joke, but it tickled old Mr Bouncer; because Tommy Brock was so fat and stumpy and grinning. So old Mr Bouncer laughed; and pressed Tommy Brock to come inside, to taste a slice of seed-cake and "a glass of my daughter Flopsy's cowslip wine". Tommy Brock squeezed himself into the rabbit hole with alacrity.

Then old Mr Bouncer smoked another pipe, and gave Tommy Brock a cabbage leaf cigar which was so very strong that it made Tommy Brock grin more than ever; and the smoke filled the burrow. Old Mr Bouncer coughed and laughed; and Tommy Brock puffed and grinned. And Mr Bouncer laughed and coughed, and shut his eyes because of the cabbage smoke …

When Flopsy and Benjamin came back – old Mr Bouncer woke up. Tommy Brock and all the young rabbit-babies had disappeared!

Mr Bouncer would not confess that he had admitted anybody into the rabbit hole. But the smell of badger was undeniable; and there were round heavy footmarks in the sand. He was in disgrace; Flopsy wrung her ears, and slapped him.

Benjamin Bunny set off at once after Tommy Brock. There was not much difficulty in tracking him; he had left his footmark and

bitter über die Knappheit an Fasaneneiern und beschuldigte Junker Voss, sie geräubert zu haben. Und die Ottern hatten alle Frösche verputzt, während er im Winter geschlafen hatte. «Ich habe seit vierzehn Tagen keine wirklich anständige Mahlzeit gehabt. Ich lebe von Erdkastanien. Ich muß Vegetarier werden und meinen eigenen Schwanz aufessen», sagte Meister Gräving.

Es war kein besonders guter Witz, doch Vater Purzel fand es ganz lustig, weil Meister Gräving so fett und stämmig war und so grinste. Also lachte Vater Purzel und überredete Meister Gräving einzutreten, um ein Stück Kümmelkuchen und ein Glas Schlüsselblumenwein von seiner Tochter Hoppeli zu probieren. Meister Gräving zwängte sich bereitwillig in den Kaninchenbau.

Dann schmauchte Vater Purzel noch ein Pfeifchen und reichte Meister Gräving eine Kohlblattzigarre, die so furchtbar stark war, daß Meister Gräving noch mehr als zuvor grinsen mußte. Der Qualm füllte den ganzen Bau. Vater Purzel lachte und hustete, und Meister Gräving paffte und grinste. Vater Purzel lachte und hustete und schloß die Augen wegen des Kohlrauchs …

Als Hoppeli und Benjamin zurückkamen, wachte Vater Purzel auf. Meister Gräving und alle kleinen Kaninchenkinder waren verschwunden.

Vater Purzel wollte nicht zugeben, daß er jemanden in den Kaninchenbau gelassen hatte. Doch der Geruch nach Dachs war nicht zu leugnen, und es gab tiefe runde Fußabdrücke im Sand. Vater Purzel fiel in Ungnade. Hoppeli rang die Ohren und gab ihm Schläge.

Benjamin Purzel eilte sofort los, um Meister Gräving zu verfolgen. Es war nicht schwierig, ihm auf die Spur zu kommen. Er hatte seine Fußabdrücke hinterlassen und war langsam den gewundenen Pfad durch

gone slowly up the winding footpath through the wood. Here he had rooted up the moss and wood sorrel. There he had dug quite a deep hole for dog darnel; and had set a mole trap. A little stream crossed the way. Benjamin skipped lightly over dry-foot; the badger's heavy steps showed plainly in the mud.

The path led to a part of the thicket where the trees had been cleared; there were leafy oak stumps, and a sea of blue hyacinths – but the smell that made Benjamin stop, was *not* the smell of flowers!

Mr Tod's stick house was before him and, for once, Mr Tod was at home. There was not only a foxey flavour in proof of it – there was smoke coming out of the broken pail that served as a chimney.

Benjamin Bunny sat up, staring; his whiskers twitched. Inside the stick house somebody dropped a plate, and said something. Benjamin stamped his foot, and bolted.

He never stopped till he came to the other side of the wood. Apparently Tommy Brock had turned the same way. Upon the top of the wall, there were again the marks of badger; and some ravellings of a sack had caught on a briar.

Benjamin climbed over the wall, into a meadow. He found another mole trap newly set; he was still upon the track of Tommy Brock. It was getting late in the afternoon. Other rabbits were coming out to enjoy the evening air. One of them in a blue coat by himself, was busily hunting for dandelions.

"Cousin Peter! Peter Rabbit, Peter Rabbit!" shouted Benjamin Bunny.

den Wald hinaufgegangen. Hier hatte er Moos und Sauerklee ausgerissen. Dort hatte er ein ziemlich tiefes Loch gemacht, um Tollgerste auszugraben; und da hatte er eine Maulwurfsfalle gesetzt. Ein Rinnsal querte den Weg. Benjamin hüpfte behend trockenen Fußes drüber weg. Die schweren Fußstapfen des Dachses waren im Matsch deutlich zu sehen.

Der Pfad führte zu einem Teil des Gehölzes, wo Bäume gefällt worden waren. Dort gab es belaubte Eichenstümpfe und ein Meer aus blauen Hyazinthen. Doch der Geruch, der Benjamin innehalten ließ, war nicht der Geruch von Blumen!

Junker Vossens Reisighaus lag vor ihm, und ausnahmsweise war Junker Voss zu Hause. Zum Beweis roch es nicht nur nach Fuchs, sondern es trat auch Rauch aus dem kaputten Eimer, der als Schornstein diente.

Benjamin Purzel richtete sich auf und starrte hinüber. Seine Barthaare zuckten. Im Reisighaus ließ jemand einen Teller fallen und sagte etwas. Benjamin stampfte mit dem Fuß auf und stürzte fort.

Er hielt nicht an, bevor er am anderen Ende des Waldes angekommen war. Offensichtlich war Meister Gräving denselben Weg gegangen. Oben auf der Mauer waren wieder die Spuren vom Dachs. Fäden von einem Sack waren an einem Brombeerstrauch hängengeblieben.

Benjamin stieg über die Mauer auf eine Wiese. Er fand wieder eine frischgesetzte Maulwurfsfalle. Er war also Meister Gräving noch auf der Spur. Es war nun schon spät am Nachmittag. Andere Kaninchen kamen hervor, um die Abendluft zu genießen. Eines in einer blauen Jacke, ganz für sich allein, suchte emsig nach Löwenzahn.

«Vetter Peter! Peter Karnickel, Peter Karnickel!» rief Benjamin Purzel.

The blue-coated rabbit sat up with pricked ears – "Whatever is the matter, Cousin Benjamin? Is it a cat? or John Stoat Ferret?"

"No, no, no! He's bagged my family – Tommy Brock – in a sack – have you seen him?"

"Tommy Brock? How many, Cousin Benjamin?"

"Seven, Cousin Peter, and all of them twins! Did he come this way? Please tell me quick!"

"Yes, yes; not ten minutes since ... he said they were *caterpillars*; I did think they were kicking rather hard, for caterpillars."

"Which way? Which way has he gone, Cousin Peter?"

"He had a sack with something 'live in it; I watched him set a mole trap. Let me use my mind, Cousin Benjamin; tell me from the beginning."

Benjamin did so.

"My Uncle Bouncer has displayed a lamentable want of discretion for his years;" said Peter reflectively, "but there are two hopeful circumstances. Your family is alive and kicking; and Tommy Brock has had refreshment. He will probably go to sleep, and keep them for breakfast."

"Which way?"

"Cousin Benjamin, compose yourself. I know very well which way. Because Mr Tod was at home in the stickhouse he has gone to Mr Tod's other house, at the top of Bull Banks. I partly know, because he offered to leave any message at Sister Cottontail's; he said he would be passing." (Cottontail had married a black rabbit, and gone to live on the hill.)

Das Kaninchen mit der blauen Jacke richtete sich auf und spitzte die Ohren. «Was gibt's, Vetter Benjamin? Etwa eine Katze oder gar Hans Hermelin-Frettchen?»

«Nein, nein! Er hat meine Kleinen gestohlen – Meister Gräving – in einem Sack – hast du ihn gesehen?»

«Meister Gräving? Wie viele denn, Vetter Benjamin?»

«Sieben, Vetter Peter, lauter Zwillinge! Ist er hier vorbeigekommen? Sag schnell!»

«Ja, ja! Vor noch nicht zehn Minuten ... er sagte, es seien Raupen. Ich dachte mir schon, daß sie ziemlich lebhaft strampelten – für Raupen.»

«Wohin? In welcher Richtung ist er gegangen, Vetter Peter?»

«Er hatte einen Sack mit was Lebendigem drin. Ich habe beobachtet, wie er eine Maulwurfsfalle setzte. Lass mich mal nachdenken, Vetter Benjamin! Erzähl von Anfang an!»

Das tat Benjamin.

«Mein Onkel Purzel hat einen für sein Alter beklagenswerten Mangel an Vorsicht gezeigt», sagte Peter nachdenklich, «doch es gibt zwei hoffnungsvolle Umstände. Deine Kleinen leben und strampeln. Und Meister Gräving hat was zu essen gehabt. Er wird sich wahrscheinlich schlafen legen und sie fürs Frühstück aufheben.»

«Wo ist er hin?»

«Vetter Benjamin, beruhige dich! Ich weiß ganz genau wohin er ist. Da Junker Voss gerade in seinem Reisighaus wohnte, ist er zu Junker Vossens anderem Haus gegangen, oben auf dem Ochsenkopf. Ich weiß es insbesondere darum, weil er mir anbot, jederzeit eine Nachricht zu Schwester Wattepusch zu bringen. Er sagte, er komme bei ihr vorbei.» (Wattepusch hatte ein schwarzes Kaninchen geheiratet und lebte jetzt auf dem Berg.)

Peter hid his dandelions, and accompanied the afflicted parent, who was all of a twitter. They crossed several fields and began to climb the hill; the tracks of Tommy Brock were plainly to be seen. He seemed to have put down the sack every dozen yards, to rest.

"He must be very puffed; we are close behind him, by the scent. What a nasty person!" said Peter.

The sunshine was still warm and slanting on the hill pastures. Half way up, Cottontail was sitting in her doorway, with four or five half-grown little rabbits playing about her; one black and the others brown.

Peter versteckte seinen Löwenzahn und begleitete den sorgenvollen Vater, der völlig aufgelöst war. Sie überquerten mehrere Felder und begannen auf den Berg zu steigen. Die Spuren von Meister Gräving waren deutlich zu sehen. Offenbar hatte er den Sack alle zehn Meter niedergesetzt, um sich auszuruhen.

«Er muß ganz außer Atem sein. Nach dem Geruch zu schließen, sind wir dicht hinter ihm. Was für ein ekelhafter Kerl!» sagte Peter.

Die Sonne schien noch warm und fiel schräg auf die Bergweiden. Auf halbem Weg nach oben saß Wattepusch vor ihrem Eingang mit vier oder fünf halbwüchsigen Kaninchenjungen, die um sie herum spielten. Eins war schwarz, die anderen waren braun.

Cottontail had seen Tommy Brock passing in the distance. Asked whether her husband was at home she replied that Tommy Brock had rested twice while she watched him. He had nodded, and pointed to the sack, and seemed doubled up with laughing.

"Come away, Peter; he will be cooking them; come quicker!" said Benjamin Bunny.

They climbed up and up.

"He was at home; I saw his black ears peeping out of the hole."

"They live too near the rocks to quarrel with their neighbours. Come on, Cousin Benjamin!"

When they came near the wood at the top of Bull Banks, they went cautiously. The trees grew amongst heaped-up rocks; and there, beneath a crag – Mr Tod had made one of his homes. It was at the top of a steep bank; the rocks and bushes overhung it. The rabbits crept up carefully, listening and peeping.

This house was something between a cave, a prison, and a tumble-down pig-stye. There was a strong door, which was shut and locked.

The setting sun made the window panes glow like red flame; but the kitchen fire was not alight. It was neatly laid with dry sticks, as the rabbits could see, when they peeped through the window.

Benjamin sighed with relief.

But there were preparations upon the kitchen table which made him shudder. There was an immense empty pie-dish of blue willow pattern, and a large carving knife and fork, and a chopper.

At the other end of the table was a partly

Wattepusch hatte Meister Gräving in der Ferne vorbeigehen sehen. Auf die Frage der beiden, ob ihr Mann zu Hause sei, antwortete sie, daß Meister Gräving zweimal gerastet habe, solange sie ihm nachsah. Er hatte ihr zugewinkt und auf den Sack gezeigt – er schien sich vor Lachen zu krümmen.

«Komm weiter, Peter! Er wird sie noch kochen! Komm schneller!» sagte Benjamin Purzel.

Sie stiegen höher und höher.

«Wattepuschs Mann war zu Hause! Ich habe seine schwarzen Ohren aus der Höhle gucken sehen.»

«Sie wohnen zu nah an den Felsen, um sich mit ihren Nachbarn anlegen zu dürfen. Komm weiter, Vetter Benjamin!»

Als sie sich dem Wald oben auf dem Ochsenkopf näherten, gingen sie vorsichtig. Die Bäume wuchsen zwischen aufgetürmten Felsen, und dort, unter einem Buckel, hatte Junker Voss eine seiner Behausungen gebaut. Sie lag oberhalb einer steilen Böschung. Felsen und Buschwerk verhängten sie. Die Kaninchen krochen vorsichtig heran, lauschten und lugten.

Die Behausung war eine Mischung aus Höhle, Gefängnis und baufälligem Schweinestall. Sie hatte eine feste Tür, die zu und abgeschlossen war.

Die untergehende Sonne ließ die Fensterscheiben wie rote Flammen aufglühen. Aber das Feuer in der Küche brannte nicht. Es war mit trockenen Scheiten säuberlich angelegt, wie die Kaninchen sehen konnten, als sie durch das Fenster spähten.

Benjamin seufzte vor Erleichterung.

Doch auf dem Küchentisch war einiges vorbereitet, was ihn schaudern machte. Da stand eine riesengroße leere Pastetenform mit blauem Weidenmuster, und daneben lagen ein langes Tranchierbesteck und ein Hackmesser.

Am anderen Ende des Tisches lag ein halb aufge-

unfolded tablecloth, a plate, a tumbler, a knife and fork, salt-cellar, mustard and a chair – in short, preparations for one person's supper.

No person was to be seen, and no young rabbits. The kitchen was empty and silent; the clock had run down. Peter and Benjamin flattened their noses against the window, and stared into the dusk. Then they scrambled round the rocks to the other side of the house. It was damp and smelly, and overgrown with thorns and briars. The rabbits shivered in their shoes.

"Oh my poor rabbit babies! What a dreadful place; I shall never see them again!" sighed Benjamin.

They crept up to the bedroom window. It was closed and bolted like the kitchen. But there were signs that this window had been

schlagenes Tischtuch und darauf gedeckt ein Teller, ein
Trinkglas, ein Messer und eine Gabel, Salzfaß, Senf
und davor ein Stuhl – kurz: Vorbereitungen für ein
Ein-Personen-Nachtmahl.

Niemand war zu sehen, auch keine jungen Kaninchen. Die Küche war leer, und es war ganz leise. Die
Uhr war abgelaufen. Peter und Benjamin drückten
ihre Nasen gegen das Fenster und starrten in das Halb-
dunkel. Dann krabbelten sie um die Felsen herum
auf die andere Seite des Hauses. Sie war feucht und
muffig und überwachsen von Dornen- und Brombeer-
gestrüpp. Den Kaninchen zitterten die Knie.

«Oh meine armen Kaninchenkinder! Was für ein
entsetzlicher Ort! Ich werde sie nie wieder sehen!»
seufzte Benjamin.

Sie krochen zum Schlafzimmerfenster hin. Es war
geschlossen und verriegelt wie die Küche. Doch es
gab Anzeichen dafür, daß dieses Fenster vor kurzem

recently open; the cobwebs were disturbed, and there were fresh dirty footmarks upon the window-sill.

The room inside was so dark, that at first they could make out nothing; but they could hear a noise – a slow deep regular snoring grunt. And as their eyes became accustomed to the darkness, they perceived that somebody was asleep on Mr Tod's bed, curled up under the blanket.

"He has gone to bed in his boots," whispered Peter.

Benjamin, who was all of a twitter, pulled Peter off the window-sill.

Tommy Brocks snores continued, grunty and regular from Mr Tod's bed. Nothing could be seen of the young family.

The sun had set; an owl began to hoot in the wood. There were many unpleasant things lying about, that had much better have been buried; rabbit bones and skulls, and chickens' legs and other horrors. It was a shocking place, and very dark.

They went back to the front of the house, and tried in every way to move the bolt of the kitchen window. They tried to push up a rusty nail between the window sashes; but it was of no use, especially without a light.

They sat side by side outside the window, whispering and listening. In half an hour the moon rose over the wood. It shone full and clear and cold, upon the house amongst the rocks, and in at the kitchen window. But alas, no little rabbit babies were to be seen!

The moonbeams twinkled on the carving knife and the pie-dish, and made a path of

offen gewesen war. Die Spinnweben waren zerstört, und auf dem Fenstersims waren frische schmutzige Fußspuren.

Der Raum innen war so dunkel, daß sie erst nichts erkennen konnten. Doch sie konnten ein Geräusch hören, ein langsames tiefes gleichmäßiges Schnarchgegrunz. Und als sich ihre Augen an die Dunkelheit gewöhnt hatten, bemerkten sie, daß jemand im Bett von Junker Voss unter der Decke zusammengerollt schlief.

«Er ist mit den Stiefeln ins Bett gegangen», flüsterte Peter.

Benjamin, der vor Angst außer sich war, zog Peter vom Fenstersims weg.

Das Schnarchen von Meister Gräving hielt an, grunzend und gleichmäßig kam es aus Junker Vossens Bett. Von den Kleinen war nichts zu sehen.

Die Sonne war untergegangen. Im Wald begann eine Eule zu rufen. Viele unerfreuliche Dinge lagen herum, die viel besser eingebuddelt gehört hätten: Kaninchenknochen und -schädel und Hühnerbeine und anderer Graus. Es war hier abscheulich und sehr finster.

Sie gingen wieder zur Vorderseite des Hauses und versuchten auf alle mögliche Weise, den Schließhaken des Küchenfensters zu verschieben. Sie versuchten, einen rostigen Nagel zwischen die Fensterrahmen hochzustoßen. Doch es ging nicht, noch dazu ohne Licht.

Sie saßen nebeneinander vor dem Fenster und flüsterten und lauschten. Nach einer halben Stunde ging der Mond über dem Wald auf. Er schien voll und klar und kühl zwischen den Felsen hindurch auf das Haus und durch das Küchenfenster hinein. Aber ach, keine kleinen Kaninchenkinder waren zu sehen!

Die Mondstrahlen glitzerten auf dem Tranchiermesser und der Pastetenform und warfen eine helle Bahn

brightness across the dirty floor. The light showed a little door in a wall beside the kitchen fireplace – a little iron door belonging to a brick oven, of that old-fashioned sort that used to be heated with faggots of wood.

And presently at the same moment Peter and Benjamin noticed that whenever they shook the window – the little door opposite shook in answer. The young family were alive; shut up in the oven!

Benjamin was so excited that it was a mercy he did not awake Tommy Brock, whose snores continued solemnly in Mr Tod's bed.

But there really was not very much comfort in the discovery. They could not open the window; and although the young family was alive – the little rabbits were quite incapable of letting themselves out; they were not old enough to crawl.

After much whispering, Peter and Benjamin decided to dig a tunnel. They began to burrow a yard or two lower down the bank. They hoped that they might be able to work between the large stones under the house; the kitchen floor was so dirty that it was impossible to say whether it was made of earth or flags.

They dug and dug for hours. They could not tunnel straight on account of stones; but by the end of the night they were under the kitchen floor. Benjamin was on his back, scratching upwards. Peter's claws were worn down; he was outside the tunnel, shuffling sand away. He called out that it was morning – sunrise; and that the jays were making a noise down below in the woods.

Benjamin Bunny came out of the dark tun-

auf den schmutzigen Fußboden. Das Licht machte eine kleine Tür in der Wand neben der Feuerstelle in der Küche sichtbar, eine kleine eiserne Tür, die zu einem gemauerten Backofen gehörte, einem von der altmodischen Art, die mit Reisigbündeln erhitzt wurden.

In diesem Augenblick bemerkten Peter und Benjamin, daß immer, wenn sie am Fenster rüttelten, als Antwort darauf die kleine Tür gegenüber rüttelte. Die Kleinen lebten, im Backofen eingeschlossen!

Benjamin war furchtbar aufgeregt. Man konnte nur von Glück reden, daß er nicht Meister Gräving weckte, der in Junker Vossens Bett ununterbrochen würdevoll weiterschnarchte.

Aber eine wirklich große Erleichterung hatte diese Entdeckung nicht gebracht. Sie konnten das Fenster nicht öffnen. Und obwohl die kleinen Kaninchen lebten – sie waren überhaupt nicht in der Lage, sich selber zu befreien. Sie waren nicht einmal alt genug, um zu krabbeln.

Nach langem Flüstern beschlossen Peter und Benjamin, einen Gang zu graben. Sie begannen, ein oder zwei Meter tiefer in der Böschung zu buddeln. Sie hofften, sich zwischen den großen Steinen unterm Haus durcharbeiten zu können. Der Küchenboden war so schmutzig, daß man unmöglich feststellen konnte, ob er aus Erde oder Fliesen bestand.

Sie gruben und gruben stundenlang. Wegen der Steine konnten sie nicht auf kürzestem Weg vorankommen. Doch am Ende der Nacht waren sie unter dem Küchenfußboden angelangt. Benjamin lag auf dem Rücken und kratzte nach oben. Peters Klauen waren abgewetzt. Er war draußen vor dem Gang und schaffte Sand beiseite. Er rief, daß der Morgen komme – Sonnenaufgang –, und daß die Eichelhäher unten in den Wäldern Krach schlügen.

Benjamin Purzel kam aus dem dunklen Gang hervor

nel, shaking the sand from his ears; he cleaned his face with his paws. Every minute the sun shone warmer on the top of the hill. In the valley there was a sea of white mist, with golden tops of trees showing through.

Again from the fields down below in the mist there came the angry cry of a jay – followed by the sharp yelping bark of a fox! Then those two rabbits lost their heads completely. They did the most foolish thing that they could have done. They rushed into their short new tunnel, and hid themselves at the top end of it, under Mr Tod's kitchen floor.

Mr Tod was coming up Bull Banks, and he was in the very worst of tempers. First he had been upset by breaking the plate. It was his own fault; but it was a china plate, the last of the dinner service that had belonged to his grandmother, old Vixen Tod. Then the midges had been very bad. And he had failed to catch a hen pheasant on her nest; and it had contained only five eggs, two of them addled. Mr Tod had had an unsatisfactory night.

As usual, when out of humour, he determined to move house. First he tried the pollard willow, but it was damp; and the otters had left a dead fish near it. Mr Tod likes nobody's leavings but his own.

He made his way up the hill; his temper was not improved by noticing unmistakable marks of badger. No one else grubs up the moss so wantonly as Tommy Brock.

Mr Tod slapped his stick upon the earth and fumed; he guessed where Tommy Brock had gone to. He was further annoyed by the jay bird which followed him persistently. It flew

und schüttelte sich den Sand aus den Ohren. Er säuberte sich das Gesicht mit den Pfoten. Mit jeder Minute schien die Sonne wärmer auf die Bergkuppe. Im Tal lag ein Meer aus weißem Nebel, aus dem goldene Baumspitzen hervorschauten.

Wieder tönte unten aus den Feldern im Nebel der ärgerliche Ruf eines Eichelhähers, gefolgt von dem harten kläffenden Gebell eines Fuchses. Da verloren die beiden Kaninchen völlig den Kopf. Sie taten das Dümmste, was sie tun konnten. Sie stürzten in ihren kurzen neuen Gang und versteckten sich am oberen Ende unter Junker Vossens Küchenfußboden.

Junker Voss kam den Ochsenkopf in allerschlechtester Laune herauf. Erstens hatte es ihn verdrossen, daß der Teller zerbrochen war. Es war zwar seine eigene Schuld, doch es war ein Porzellanteller, der letzte aus einem Tafelgeschirr, das seiner Großmutter, der alten Fähe Voss, gehört hatte. Zweitens waren die Stechmücken besonders schlimm gewesen. Drittens war es ihm mißlungen, eine Fasanenhenne auf ihrem Nest zu schnappen. Und das Nest hatte nur fünf Eier enthalten, von denen zwei faul waren. Junker Voss hatte eine unbefriedigende Nacht gehabt.

Wie üblich, wenn er mißmutig war, wollte er die Unterkunft wechseln. Erst versuchte er es bei der gestutzten Weide, doch da war es feucht. Und die Ottern hatten nahebei einen toten Fisch liegenlassen. Junker Voss mag niemandes Abfälle außer seinen eigenen.

Er schlug den Weg zum Berg ein. Seine Laune wurde nicht besser, als er unverkennbare Spuren von einem Dachs bemerkte. Kein anderer wühlt das Moos so liederlich auf wie Meister Gräving.

Junker Voss stieß mit dem Stock auf den Boden; er kochte innerlich. Er ahnte, wohin Meister Gräving gegangen war. Außerdem wurde er belästigt von dem Eichelhäher, der ihm hartnäckig folgte. Der flog

from tree to tree and scolded, warning every rabbit within hearing that either a cat or a fox was coming up the plantation. Once when it flew screaming over his head – Mr Tod snapped at it, and barked.

He approached his house very carefully, with a large rusty key. He sniffed and his whiskers bristled. The house was locked up, but Mr Tod had his doubts whether it was empty. He turned the rusty key in the lock; the rabbits below could hear it. Mr Tod opened the door cautiously and went in.

The sight that met Mr Tod's eyes in Mr Tod's kitchen made Mr Tod furious. There was Mr Tod's chair, and Mr Tod's pie-dish, and his knife and fork and mustard and salt-cellar and his tablecloth that he had left folded up in the dresser – all set out for supper (or break-fast) – without doubt for that odious Tommy Brock.

There was a smell of fresh earth and dirty badger, which fortunately overpowered all smell of rabbit.

But what absorbed Mr Tod's attention was a noise – a deep slow regular snoring grunting noise, coming from his own bed. He peeped through the hinges of the half-open bedroom door. Then he turned and came out of the house in a hurry. His whiskers bristled and his coat-collar stood on end with rage.

For the next twenty minutes Mr Tod kept creeping cautiously into the house, and re-treating hurriedly out again. By degrees he ventured further in – right into the bedroom. When he was outside the house, he scratched up the earth with fury. But when he was inside

schimpfend von Baum zu Baum und warnte so jedes Kaninchen in Hörweite, daß entweder eine Katze oder ein Fuchs den Schonwald heraufkam. Als er einmal kreischend über seinen Kopf flog, schnappte Junker Voss nach ihm und blaffte.

Er näherte sich sehr vorsichtig seinem Haus mit einem großen rostigen Schlüssel. Er schnüffelte umher und seine Barthaare sträubten sich. Das Haus war zwar abgeschlossen, doch Junker Voss hatte Zweifel, ob es auch leer war. Er drehte den rostigen Schlüssel im Schloß. Die Kaninchen unten konnten es hören. Junker Voss öffnete behutsam die Tür und trat ein.

Der Anblick, der sich Junker Voss in Junker Vossens Küche bot, machte Junker Voss rasend. Dort war Junker Vossens Stuhl und Junker Vossens Pasteten-form und sein Besteck und sein Senf und sein Salzfaß und sein Tischtuch, das er zusammengefaltet in die Anrichte gelegt hatte – alles zum Abendessen (oder Frühstück) hergerichtet – ohne Zweifel für den ver-haßten Meister Gräving.

Es roch nach frischer Erde und schmutzigem Dachs, der zum Glück allen Kaninchengeruch überdeckte.

Doch die Aufmerksamkeit von Junker Voss wurde von einem Geräusch in Anspruch genommen, einem tiefen langsamen gleichmäßigen schnarchenden Grunzgeräusch, das aus seinem eigenen Bett kam. Er spähte durch den Angelspalt der halbgeöffneten Schlaf-zimmertür. Dann machte er kehrt und trat eilig aus dem Haus. Sein Bart sträubte sich, und sein Jacken-kragen stand vor Wut zu Berge.

Während der nächsten zwanzig Minuten schlich Junker Voss immer wieder vorsichtig in sein Haus und zog sich immer wieder eilends zurück. Nach und nach wagte er sich weiter hinein, bis ganz ins Schlafzimmer. Wenn er außerhalb des Hauses war, scharrte er vor Zorn die Erde auf, war er aber drinnen, mißbehagte

– he did not like the look of Tommy Brock's teeth. He was lying on his back with his mouth open, grinning from ear to ear. He snored peacefully and regularly; but one eye was not perfectly shut.

Mr Tod came in and out of the bedroom. Twice he brought in his walking-stick, and once he brought in the coal-scuttle. But he thought better of it, and took them away. When he came back after removing the coal-scuttle, Tommy Brock was lying a little more sideways; but he seemed even sounder asleep. He was an incurably indolent person; he was not in the least afraid of Mr Tod; he was simply too lazy and comfortable to move.

Mr Tod came back yet again into the bedroom with a clothes line. He stood a minute watching Tommy Brock and listening attentively to the snores. They were very loud indeed, but seemed quite natural.

ihm der Anblick von Meister Grävings Zähnen. Der lag mit offenem Mund auf dem Rücken und grinste von einem Ohr bis zum anderen. Er schnarchte friedlich und gleichmäßig, doch ein Auge war nicht ganz geschlossen.

Junker Voss ging rein ins Schlafzimmer und ging wieder raus. Zweimal brachte er seinen Spazierstock mit und einmal den Kohlenkübel. Doch er überlegte es sich anders und nahm beide wieder mit hinaus. Als er wieder hineinging, nachdem er den Kohlenkübel hinausgetragen hatte, lag Meister Gräving etwas mehr auf der Seite. Doch er schien noch tiefer zu schlafen. Er war ein unverbesserlich träger Kerl und hatte nicht die geringste Angst vor Junker Voss. Er war einfach nur zu faul und lag zu bequem, um sich zu rühren.

Junker Voss trat schon wieder ins Schlafzimmer, diesmal mit einem Wäscheseil. Eine Minute lang stand er da und beobachtete Meister Gräving und lauschte angespannt auf das Schnarchen. Es war wirklich sehr laut, doch wirkte es ganz natürlich.

Mr Tod turned his back towards the bed, and undid the window. It creaked; he turned round with a jump. Tommy Brock, who had opened one eye – shut it hastily. The snores continued.

Mr Tod's proceedings were peculiar, and rather uneasy (because the bed was between the window and the door of the bedroom). He opened the window a little way, and pushed out the greater part of the clothes line on to the window-sill. The rest of the line, with a hook at the end, remained in his hand. Tommy Brock snored conscientiously. Mr Tod stood and looked at him for a minute; then he left the room again.

Tommy Brock opened both eyes, and looked at the rope and grinned. There was a noise outside the window. Tommy Brock shut his eyes in a hurry.

Mr Tod had gone out at the front door, and round to the back of the house. On the way, he stumbled over the rabbit burrow. If he had had any idea who was inside it, he would have pulled them out quickly. His foot went through the tunnel nearly upon the top of Peter Rabbit and Benjamin, but fortunately he thought that it was some more of Tommy Brock's work.

He took up the coil of line from the sill, listened for a moment, and then tied the rope to a tree.

Tommy Brock watched him with one eye, through the window. He was puzzled.

Mr Tod fetched a large heavy pailful of water from the spring, and staggered with it through the kitchen into his bedroom.

Tommy Brock snored industriously, with rather a snort.

Junker Voss wandte dem Bett den Rücken zu und entriegelte das Fenster. Es quietschte. Mit einem Satz drehte er sich um. Meister Gräving, der ein Auge geöffnet hatte, schloß es schnellstens. Das Schnarchen ging weiter.

Das Vorgehen von Junker Voss war gewagt, und ihm war gar nicht sehr wohl dabei (weil das Bett zwischen dem Fenster und der Schlafzimmertür stand). Er öffnete das Fenster einen kleinen Spalt und schob das längere Ende des Wäscheseils auf das Fenstersims. Den Rest des Seils, an dessen Ende ein Haken war, behielt er in der Hand. Meister Gräving schnarchte gewissenhaft. Junker Voss stand und beobachtete ihn eine Minute lang. Dann ging er wieder aus dem Zimmer.

Meister Gräving öffnete beide Augen, blickte auf das Seil und grinste. Von draußen vorm Fenster kam ein Geräusch. Sogleich schloß Meister Gräving die Augen.

Junker Voss war aus der Haustür und ums Haus herum nach der Rückseite gegangen. Dabei stolperte er über das Kaninchenloch. Wenn er geahnt hätte, wer dort drinnen steckte, hätte er die beiden rasch herausgezogen. Sein Fuß trat durch den Stollengang fast auf Peter Karnickels und Benjamins Köpfe, doch zum Glück glaubte er, daß dies auch noch so ein Machwerk von Meister Gräving sei.

Er nahm das aufgerollte Seil vom Fenstersims, lauschte noch eine Weile und band dann das Seil an einen Baum.

Meister Gräving beobachtete ihn mit einem Auge durchs Fenster und wunderte sich.

Junker Voss holte einen großen schweren Eimer mit Wasser von der Quelle und wankte damit durch die Küche ins Schlafzimmer.

Meister Gräving schnarchte fleißig, jetzt ziemlich schnaubend.

Mr Tod put down the pail beside the bed, took up the end of rope with the hook – hesitated, and looked at Tommy Brock. The snores were almost apoplectic; but the grin was not quite so big.

Mr Tod gingerly mounted a chair by the head of the bedstead. His legs were dangerously near to Tommy Brock's teeth. He reached up und put the end of rope, with the hook, over the head of the tester bed, where the curtains ought to hang. (Mr Tod's curtains were folded up, and put away, owing to the house being unoccupied. So was the counterpane. Tommy Brock was covered with a blanket only). Mr Tod standing on the unsteady chair looked down upon him attentively; he really was a first prize sound sleeper! It seemed as though nothing would waken him – not even the flapping rope across the bed.

Mr Tod descended safely from the chair, and endeavoured to get up again with the pail of water. He intended to hang it from the hook, dangling over the head of Tommy Brock, in order to make a sort of shower-bath, worked by a string, through the window.

But naturally being a thin-legged person (though vindictive and sandy whiskered) – he was quite unable to lift the heavy weight to the level of the hook and rope. He very nearly overbalanced himself.

The snores became more and more apoplectic. One of Tommy Brock's hind legs twitched under the blanket, but still he slept on peacefully.

Mr Tod and the pail descended from the chair without accident. After considerable

Junker Voss stellte den Eimer neben das Bett, nahm das Ende des Seils auf, an dem der Haken war, zögerte und blickte auf Meister Gräving. Das Schnarchen kam jetzt in unruhigen Stößen, doch das Grinsen war nicht mehr ganz so breit.

Junker Voss stieg behutsam auf einen Stuhl am Kopfende der Bettstatt. Seine Beine waren gefährlich nahe bei Meister Grävings Zähnen. Er reckte sich und hängte das Ende des Seils mit dem Haken über den Baldachin des Himmelbetts, an dem eigentlich Vorhänge sein sollten. Junker Vossens Vorhänge waren zusammengefaltet und weggeräumt, weil das Haus nicht bewohnt war. Ebenso verhielt es sich mit dem Federbett. (Meister Gräving lag nur unter einer Wolldecke.) Junker Voss stand auf dem wackeligen Stuhl und blickte prüfend auf Meister Gräving hinunter. Als Tiefschläfer war er wirklich erstklassig. Es schien, als ob nichts ihn wecken könne – nicht einmal das schwingende Seil über dem Bett.

Junker Voss stieg unversehrt vom Stuhl und wollte mit dem Eimer Wasser wieder hinauf. Er beabsichtigte, ihn an den Haken zu hängen, so daß er genau über Meister Grävings Kopf baumelte; es sollte so etwas wie ein Brausebad werden, das mit der Schnur durchs Fenster zu betätigen wäre.

Doch von Natur aus dünnbeinig (wenn auch rachsüchtig und mit rotbraunem Bart), war er überhaupt nicht in der Lage, das schwere Gewicht bis zur Höhe des Hakens am Seil zu heben. Er geriet fast aus dem Gleichgewicht.

Das Schnarchen kam in immer unruhigeren Stößen. Eines von Meister Grävings Hinterbeinen zuckte unter der Decke, doch noch immer schlief er friedlich weiter.

Junker Voss kam mitsamt dem Eimer, ohne zu verunglücken, vom Stuhl herunter. Nach reiflicher

thought, he emptied the water into a wash-basin and jug. The empty pail was not too heavy for him; he slung it up wobbling over the head of Tommy Brock.

Surely there never was such a sleeper! Mr Tod got up and down, down and up on the chair. As he could not lift the whole pailful of water at once, he fetched a milk jug and ladled quarts of water into the pail by degrees. The pail got fuller and fuller, and swung like a pendulum. Occasionally a drop splashed over; but still Tommy Brock snored regularly and never moved, – except one eye.

Überlegung goß er das Wasser in eine Waschschüssel und einen Krug. Der leere Eimer war für ihn nicht zu schwer. Er hängte ihn auf – jetzt baumelte er über Meister Grävings Kopf.

Gewiß hatte es noch nie einen solchen Schläfer gegeben! Junker Voss stieg den Stuhl rauf und runter, runter und rauf. Da er nicht alles Wasser auf einmal hochheben konnte, holte er sich einen Milchkrug und goß es literweise in den Eimer. Der Eimer wurde voller und voller und schwang wie ein Pendel. Gelegentlich spritzte ein Tropfen über den Rand, doch noch immer schnarchte Meister Gräving gleichmäßig und bewegte sich keinmal – ausgenommen das eine Auge.

At last Mr Tod's preparations were complete. The pail was full of water; the rope was tightly strained over the top of the bed, and across the window-sill to the tree outside. "It will make a great mess in my bedroom; but I could never sleep in that bed again without a spring cleaning of some sort," said Mr Tod.

Mr Tod took a last look at the badger and softly left the room. He went out of the house, shutting the front door. The rabbits heard his footsteps over the tunnel. He ran round behind the house, intending to undo the rope in order to let fall the pailful of water upon Tommy Brock – "I will wake him up with an unpleasant surprise," said Mr Tod.

The moment he had gone, Tommy Brock got up in a hurry; he rolled Mr Tod's dressing-gown into a bundle, put it into the bed beneath the pail of water instead of himself, and left the room also – grinning immensely. He went into the kitchen, lighted the fire and boiled the kettle; for the moment he did not trouble himself to cook the baby rabbits.

When Mr Tod go to the tree, he found that the weight and strain had dragged the knot so tight that it was past untying. He was obliged to gnaw it with his teeth. He chewed and gnawed for more than twenty minutes. At last the rope gave way with such a sudden jerk that it nearly pulled his teeth out, and quite knocked him over backwards.

Inside the house there was a great crash and splash, and the noise of a pail rolling over and over. But no screams. Mr Tod was mystified; he sat quite still, and listened attentively. Then he peeped in at the window. The water was

Endlich waren Junker Vossens Vorbereitungen abgeschlossen. Der Eimer war mit Wasser gefüllt, das Seil lief fest gespannt über den Baldachin des Bettes und übers Fenstersims nach draußen zum Baum. «Das wird in meinem Schlafzimmer eine große Schweinerei anrichten, doch ich könnte sowieso nicht mehr in diesem Bett schlafen ohne irgendeinen Frühjahrsputz», sagte sich Junker Voss.

Er warf einen letzten Blick auf den Dachs und verließ leise das Zimmer und ging aus dem Haus und schloß die Haustür. Die Kaninchen hörten seine Tritte über ihrem Gang. Junker Voss lief hinter das Haus, um das Seil zu lösen, damit der Eimer Wasser auf Meister Gräving niederginge. «Ich werde ihn mit einer unangenehmen Überraschung wecken», sagte Junker Voss.

Sowie er gegangen war, stand Meister Gräving in aller Eile auf. Er rollte Junker Vossens Morgenrock zu einem Bündel zusammen, legte ihn an seiner Statt unter den Eimer mit Wasser ins Bett und verließ auch das Zimmer – ungeheuerlich grinsend. Er ging in die Küche, zündete das Feuer an und setzte den Wasserkessel auf. Im Augenblick legte er keinen Wert darauf, die Kaninchenkinder zu kochen.

Als Junker Voss zum Baum kam, mußte er feststellen, daß das Gewicht und die Spannung den Knoten so festgezurrt hatten, daß er nicht zu lösen war. Er mußte ihn mit den Zähnen zernagen. Länger als zwanzig Minuten kaute und nagte er. Schließlich gab das Seil mit so einem plötzlichen Ruck nach, daß es ihm fast die Zähne ausriß und ihn tatsächlich nach hinten umwarf.

Innen im Haus war ein mächtiges Krachen und Platschen zu hören und das Geräusch von einem Eimer, der hin- und herrollte. Doch keine Schreie. Junker Voss war verblüfft. Er saß unbeweglich und lauschte gespannt. Dann spähte er durchs Fenster hinein. Das

dripping from the bed, the pail had rolled into a corner.

In the middle of the bed under the blanket, was a wet flattened *something* – much dinged in, in the middle where the pail had caught it (as it were across the tummy.) Its head was covered by the wet blanket and it was *not snoring any longer.*

There was nothing stirring, and no sound except the drip, drop, drop drip of water trickling from the mattress.

Mr Tod watched it for half an hour; his eyes glistened. Then he cut a caper, and became so bold that he even tapped at the window; but the bundle never moved. Yes – there was no doubt about it – it had turned out even better than he had planned; the pail had hit poor old Tommy Brock, and killed him dead!

"I will bury that nasty person in the hole which he has dug. I will bring my bedding out, and dry it in the sun," said Mr Tod. "I will wash the tablecloth and spread it on the grass in the sun to bleach. And the blanket must be hung up in the wind; and the bed must be thoroughly disinfected, and aired with a warming-pan; and warmed with a hot-water bottle. I will get soft soap, and monkey soap, and all sorts of soap; and soda and scrubbing brushes; and persian powder; and carbolic to remove the smell. I must have a disinfecting. Perhaps I may have to burn sulphur."

He hurried round the house to get a shovel from the kitchen – "First I will arrange the hole – then I will drag out that person in the blanket ..."

He opened the door ...

Wasser tropfte vom Bett herab. Der Eimer war in eine Ecke gerollt.

Mitten im Bett unter der Decke lag etwas flaches Nasses – im Mittelteil, wo der Eimer aufgetroffen war, ziemlich eingedrückt, sozusagen in der Bauchgegend. Der Kopf von diesem flachen nassen Etwas befand sich unter der nassen Decke, und das Etwas schnarchte nicht mehr.

Nichts rührte sich, und nichts war zu hören als das Tropf-Tropf, Tropf-Tropf des Wassers, das von der Matratze tröpfelte.

Junker Voss beobachtete das eine halbe Stunde lang. Seine Augen funkelten. Dann machte er einen Freudensprung und wurde so kühn, daß er sogar ans Fenster pochte. Doch das Bündel rührte sich nicht. Ja – kein Zweifel – es war noch glücklicher ausgegangen, als er geplant hatte. Der Eimer hatte den armen alten Meister Gräving getroffen und ihm den Garaus gemacht.

«Den widerwärtigen Kerl begrabe ich in dem Loch, das er gebuddelt hat. Mein Bettzeug bringe ich heraus und lasse es in der Sonne trocknen», sagte Junker Voss. «Mein Tischtuch wasche ich und lege es in der Sonne aufs Gras zum Bleichen. Die Wolldecke muß in den Wind gehängt werden. Und das Bett muß gründlich desinfiziert und mit einer Wärmpfanne getrocknet und mit einer Wärmflasche gewärmt werden. Ich werde Schmierseife und Scheuerseife besorgen, alle möglichen Sorten von Seifen, und Soda und Schrubbbürsten und Flit und auch Karbol, um den Geruch wegzubringen. Ich muß ein keimtötendes Mittel verwenden. Vielleicht werde ich sogar Schwefel abbrennen müssen.»

Er eilte ums Haus herum, um aus der Küche eine Schaufel zu holen. «Erst muß ich das Loch vorbereiten und dann den Kerl mit der Decke herausschleifen ...»

Er öffnete die Tür ...

Tommy Brock was sitting at Mr Tod's kitchen table, pouring out tea from Mr Tod's tea-pot into Mr Tod's tea-cup. He was quite dry himself and grinning; and he threw the cup of scalding tea all over Mr Tod.

Then Mr Tod rushed upon Tommy Brock, and Tommy Brock grappled with Mr Tod amongst the broken crockery, and there was a terrific battle all over the kitchen.

To the rabbits underneath it sounded as if the floor would give way at each crash of falling furniture. They crept out of their tunnel, and hung about amongst the rocks and bushes, listening anxiously.

Inside the house the racket was fearful. The rabbit babies in the oven woke up trembling; perhaps it was fortunate they were shut up inside.

Meister Gräving saß an Junker Vossens Küchentisch und goß sich aus Junker Vossens Teekanne Tee in Junker Vossens Teetasse. Er selber war vollkommen trocken und grinste. Dann warf er die Tasse mit dem kochend heißem Tee nach Junker Voss.

Da stürzte sich Junker Voss auf Meister Gräving, und Meister Gräving und Junker Voss rauften miteinander zwischen dem zerbrochenen Geschirr. Eine gewaltige Schlacht tobte durch die ganze Küche.

Für die Kaninchen darunter klang es, als ob der Fußboden bei jedem Poltern eines umstürzenden Möbels nachgäbe. Sie krochen aus ihrem Gang und drückten sich ängstlich lauschend zwischen den Felsen und Büschen herum.

Der Lärm innen im Haus war fürchterlich. Die Kaninchenkinder im Backofen erwachten zitternd. Vielleicht war es ein Glück, daß sie drinnen eingeschlossen waren.

Everything was upset except the kitchen table. And everything was broken, except the mantelpiece and the kitchen fender. The crockery was smashed to atoms. The chairs were broken, and the window, and the clock fell with a crash, and there were handfuls of Mr Tod's sandy whiskers. The vases fell off the shelf; the kettle fell off the hob. Tommy Brock put his foot in a jar of raspberry jam. And the boiling water out of the kettle fell upon the tail of Mr Tod.

When the kettle fell, Tommy Brock, who was still grinning, happened to be uppermost; and he rolled Mr Tod over and over like a log, out at the door. Then the snarling and worrying went on outside; and they rolled over the bank, and down hill, bumping over the rocks. There will never be any love lost between Tommy Brock and Mr Tod.

As soon as the coast was clear, Peter Rabbit and Benjamin Bunny came out of the bushes –

"Now for it! Run in, Cousin Benjamin! Run in and get them! while I watch at the door."

But Benjamin was frightened – "Oh; oh! they are coming back!"

No they are not."

"Yes they are!"

"What dreadful bad language! I think they have fallen down the stone quarry."

Still Benjamin hesitated, and Peter kept pushing him – "Be quick, it's all right. Shut the oven door, Cousin Benjamin, so that he won't miss them."

Decidedly there were lively doings in Mr Tod's kitchen!

Bis auf den Küchentisch wurde alles umgeworfen. Und bis auf den Kaminsims und das Kamingitter wurde alles zerschlagen. Das Geschirr zerbrach in tausend Stücke. Die Stühle und das Fenster wurden zertrümmert, und die Standuhr stürzte mit einem Krach um, und büschelweise lagen rotbraune Barthaare von Junker Voss herum. Die Vasen fielen vom Kaminsims, die Blechdosen fielen vom Regal. Der Wasserkessel fiel vom Kamineinsatz. Meister Gräving trat in ein Glas Himbeermarmelade. Das kochende Wasser aus dem Kessel spritzte auf den Schwanz von Junker Voss.

Als der Kessel herunterfiel, hatte Meister Gräving, der immer noch grinste, gerade die Oberhand und er rollte Junker Voss wie einen Holzklotz über den Boden und aus der Tür hinaus. Dann ging das Fauchen und Würgen draußen weiter. Sie rollten die Böschung hinunter und holterdipolter ging es bergab über die Felsen. Meister Gräving und Junker Voss sind ein für allemal miteinander fertig.

Sobald die Luft rein war, kamen Peter Karnickel und Benjamin Purzel aus den Büschen heraus.

«Nun aber los! Lauf hinein, Vetter Benjamin! Lauf hinein und hol sie! Ich halte an der Tür Wache.»

Doch Benjamin hatte Angst. «Oh, oh! Sie kommen zurück!»

«Nein, das tun sie nicht!»

«Doch, das tun sie!»

«Wie schrecklich sie fluchen! Ich glaube, sie sind den Steinbruch hinuntergestürzt.»

Benjamin zögerte immer noch, und Peter hörte nicht auf, ihn anzutreiben. «Mach schnell, es klappt schon! Mach die Backofentür wieder zu, Vetter Benjamin, damit er sie nicht gleich vermißt!»

Wahrhaftig, in Junker Vossens Küche geschahen wirklich aufregende Sachen.

At home in the rabbit hole, things had not been quite comfortable. After quarrelling at supper, Flopsy and old Mr Bouncer had passed a sleepless night, and quarrelled again at breakfast. Old Mr Bouncer could no longer deny that he had invited company into the rabbit hole; but he refused to reply to the questions and reproaches of Flopsy. The day passed heavily.

Old Mr Bouncer, very sulky, was huddled up in a corner, barricaded with a chair. Flopsy had taken away his pipe and hidden the tobacco. She had been having a complete turn out and spring-cleaning, to relieve her feelings. She had just finished. Old Mr Bouncer, behind his chair, was wondering anxiously what she would do next.

In Mr Tod's kitchen, amongst the wreckage, Benjamin Bunny picked his way to the oven nervously, through a thick cloud of dust. He opened the oven door, felt inside, and found something warm and wriggling. He lifted it out carefully, and rejoined Peter Rabbit.

"I've got them! Can we get away? Shall we hide, Cousin Peter?"

Peter pricked his ears; distant sounds of fighting still echoed in the wood.

Five minutes afterwards two breathless rabbits came scuttering away down Bull Banks, half carrying, half dragging a sack between them, bumpetty bump over the grass. They reached home safely and burst into the rabbit hole.

Great was old Mr Bouncer's relief and Flopsy's joy when Peter and Benjamin arrived

Zu Hause im Kaninchenbau war es auch nicht gerade gemütlich zugegangen. Beim Abendessen hatten sich Hoppeli und Vater Purzel gestritten, dann hatten sie eine schlaflose Nacht verbracht und beim Frühstück wieder gestritten. Vater Purzel konnte nicht länger leugnen, daß er sich Gesellschaft in den Kaninchenbau geladen hatte. Doch er lehnte es ab, auf die Fragen und Vorwürfe von Hoppeli einzugehen. Der Tag verlief beklommen.

Vater Purzel kauerte äußerst mürrisch in einer Ecke, hinter einem Stuhl verschanzt. Hoppeli hatte ihm die Pfeife weggenommen und den Tabak versteckt. Sie hatte das Zimmer völlig ausgeräumt und Frühjahrsputz gehalten, um ihren Gefühlen Luft zu machen. Gerade war sie fertig geworden. Vater Purzel hinter seinem Stuhl fragte sich bange, was ihr als nächstes einfallen würde.

In Junker Vossens Küche bahnte sich Benjamin Purzel in einer dichten Staubwolke ängstlich seinen Weg zwischen den Trümmern zum Backofen. Er öffnete die Backofentür, tastete hinein und fühlte etwas Warmes, Zappelndes. Er hob es vorsichtig heraus und kam zu Peter zurück.

«Ich hab sie! Können wir nun entkommen? Oder sollen wir uns verstecken, Vetter Peter?»

Peter spitzte die Ohren. Das Echo von fernen Kampfgeräuschen hallte immer noch durch den Wald.

Fünf Minuten später kamen zwei atemlose Kaninchen den Ochsenkopf hinunter- und davongehastet. Halb trugen sie, halb zogen sie einen Sack zwischen sich her, hopsala hopp, über den Grasboden. Sie kamen heil daheim an und stürmten in den Kaninchenbau.

Groß waren Vater Purzels Erleichterung und Hoppelis Freude, als sich Peter und Benjamin siegreich mit

in triumph with the young family. The rabbit-babies were rather tumbled and very hungry; they were fed and put to bed. They soon recovered.

A long new pipe and a fresh supply of rabbit tobacco was presented to Mr Bouncer. He was rather upon his dignity; but he accepted.

Old Mr Bouncer was forgiven, and they all had dinner. Then Peter and Benjamin told their story – but they had not waited long enough to be able to tell the end of the battle between Tommy Brock and Mr Tod.

den Kleinen einfanden. Die Kaninchenkinder waren ziemlich durchgeschüttelt und sehr hungrig. Sie wurden gefüttert und ins Bett gebracht. Sie erholten sich schnell.

Eine lange neue Pfeife und frischer Vorrat an Kaninchentabak wurde Vater Purzel dargereicht. Er gab sich ziemlich unnahbar, doch er nahm es an.

Sie hatten Vater Purzel verziehen und setzten sich nun alle zu Tisch. Da erzählten Peter und Benjamin ihre Geschichte – sie hatten nur nicht lange genug gewartet, um den Ausgang des Kampfes zwischen Meister Gräving und Junker Voss erzählen zu können.